Allsorts

Of short stories and poems

<u>Deborah Carter</u>

ISBN 978-0-473-51570-6
ISBN 978-0-473-51571-3

Cover art & illustrations by Steve Carter

Facebook;	@debbiecarter27
Twitter;	@CDeborah6
Instagram;	@debbiecarter27
Website;	www.deborahcarterauthor.com
Email;	authordeborahcarter@gmail.com

Allsorts

A compilation of short stories and poems.

Dedicated to the Ashburton Writers Group.

Thank you for all the encouragement.

Rae, Julie, Stacey and Deirdre

Ashburton Writers Group holds a monthly meeting, and we have an assignment to complete for each gathering. Some of the following stories and poems are from these assignments.

Contents

Chi

Prologue

Green dusty feathers fan as Chi spreads her wings and flaps. She was so close to being airborne, and I watched her with such deep concentration, silently willing her to take flight, that I totally forgot the old, balding fat man between my thighs.

Chi was the orphanage's pet lorikeet, my inspiration and my only friend. I could talk to Chi; cry my tears onto her dusty feathers as she paraded up and down my arm, claws clinging for dear life to the ragged sleeve of my cardigan. Like all the inmates here, Chi had been abandoned, left alone to die in a cage no bigger than a shoebox. Chi was saved only by the orphaned children pleading for a pet to bring a little joy and life to the old rundown building, but lorikeets are a one-person kind of bird and lucky for me, I was her chosen one. I could pet her, carry her around without her biting and ripping through my skin with her sharp beak as she was wont to do with any other who put their hands near her cage, and so I became her sole carer. I cleaned out her tiny space, fed her from my meagre rations and kept her water clean. As I said, she was my friend! She was an inspiration, as she perched on a simple wooden doweling, preening, never letting the tiny space she was enclosed in stop her from being herself, from being beautiful; as she cleansed the dust from her magnificent forest green feathers and bright orange head until she shone. She twittered to herself, whistled her nonsensical tunes and squawked loud and painful at anyone who entered the dorm room. Her clipped wings kept her caged even as I showed her the semblance of freedom, going against the rules, and opening her tiny door to allow her to stretch and stomp, and as she bobbed her head happily up and down, I rediscovered my smile.

I can barely remember when smiling was a spontaneous gaiety which had been a part of my life. I mourned my parents and my baby brother daily, even after all this time. Who could have thought a driver, drunk at 8.30 a.m. and speeding past the school as my folks dropped me off ready for another day of classroom drama would have resulted in their deaths; three coffins lowered into the dirt and a social worker took me and my small suitcase to the orphanage, my new home.

Chapter one

At the tender age of twelve, my life turned upside down. I was led down the grungy passageway and delivered into the clutches of a hard-faced woman. She didn't even raise her head as we entered, just lifted her eyes from the computer screen momentarily stabbing me with a dark, hard glare and then sat back in her high-backed chair and crossed one foot over the other on the desktop; slightly raising one brow as I stood before her and continued to sob.

"Name and age?" she snapped and made me jump and cry, if possible, even harder.

"Lottie, 12," the social worker responded and placed my bag on the desk alongside a file and then she turned and left; Left me standing alone with this mean-looking woman still staring at me. She leant forward and grasped an old copper coloured bell from her desk and gave it a none to gentle shake and within seconds, a skinny girl with long greasy hair appeared from the door behind the woman.

"Alice, find her a bed in your dorm," she scowled, and the girl beckoned me to follow.

I moved forward to collect my bag when she slammed her hand on the desk.

"Leave it!" she yelled.

"But it's all my clothes and my ..." I started.

"I said, 'Leave it', you'll get what I think you need, now go," she growled.

With a heavy heart, I'd shuffled past my belongings on the desk and followed the girl through the rear door, all I had in the world was in that bag, my clothes, some of mum's trinkets I wanted for keepsakes, books and pens, but most importantly, photographs of my family. If I'd known back then that she wouldn't return it to me, I would have fought harder to hold onto it all.

Alice, my escort, led me down a passageway which ended with two doors. She moved to the left and turned the handle and walked me past bunk beds three high on either side of the room, each containing a pillow and a grey blanket spread over a grey sheet. I looked left and right as I counted eighteen beds in all as Alice stopped beside two empty mattresses.

"Take your pick," she said as she turned and reached below the end bunk and retrieved and handed me a bulky blanket. Unwrapping the bundle, I discovered a sheet and pillow inside. "Dinner is at six; I'll come to get you." And with that, I was left alone in the long, cold and lonely room. I made up my bed on the second level and crawled under the blanket and sobbed.

I didn't cope well in my new home. I spent most of my time with tears on my cheeks from missing my family so much. I caused no trouble, keeping very much to myself. We had lessons every day, the tutor being none other than Ms Finch, the hard-faced woman who stole my belongings, I hated her, but from what I overheard, everyone did. The only person I spoke to was Alice; we weren't friends, but at least we acknowledged each other, and I appreciated that she took the time to show me where I needed to be for meals and lessons and her help with chores I'd not done before. She was who I sat beside on our once a week outing to the nearby church. One night I was awoken by gentle sobbing, and I left my bunk to wander along the sleeping girls to discover the sounds coming from Alice.

"Alice," I hissed "What's wrong?" as if anything could be right in this god-awful place.

In the dim light coming through the small, dirty glass window above the door, I looked where she pointed and found a dark stain on her bedsheet.

"Did you wet the bed?" I whispered.

She shook her head, no. "It, it's blood, I'm bleeding!" she stammered.

"I'll go get Finch," I said and headed for the door. The stony-faced woman was frightening during daylight hours but waking her in the dead of night was not something I would wish to do again. Her angry "What the fuck, whose out of bed?" came to my ears as I knocked tentatively on her door.

"It's me Ms Finch, Lottie." The door swung open. "There's something wrong with Alice; she's bleeding."

Ms Finch smiled or grimaced, it was hard to tell, but she walked swiftly to our dorm with me trailing behind. "Come." She ordered, and I watched as Alice left the dorm and closed the door behind them. Alice didn't come back that night or the next, even though I lay listening for the door. I wondered if she'd maybe died from all the bleeding but was sure someone would have said something. Hey, maybe she'd been fostered or adopted, that would be a dream come true for us all. That happy thought disintegrated when I caught sight of Alice a few days later coming from the door to the right. I didn't understand why she'd changed rooms. I'd never seen inside the other room; the door never seemed to be open, and the girls who lived in there worked to a different timetable than we did in the left room. I'd seen them occasionally walking past the window while we sat at lessons, but they never interacted with us younger kids. I didn't realise that Alice's bleeding that night had made her one of the older kids now, but it was a lesson I was to learn soon enough for myself.

I tried to catch her eye a few times during the church services we attended each Sunday evening. The younger girls, all dressed in Sunday smocks and the oversized coats, which were truly needed as we walked along the cobbled street in the freezing weather. We'd enter the church doors and stomp our sodden feet or knock snow from our thin shoes before entering and sitting in our designated pews. The older girls sat down the opposite side of the church in their pretty frocks, tights and boots. They sat demurely, hands on their knees and faces averted from us, silently watching the congregation and only smiling if they were spoken to by any ladies and gentlemen who approached. I was a little jealous if truth be told and I couldn't wait until I was grown up enough to move to the 'right' room so I could wear a pretty dress and warm boots and sit so nicely in church.

Be careful what you wish!

Chapter two

I'd recently turned fourteen when I was startled by a bloody show in my panties. I padded them up with toilet tissue and went in search of Ms Finch.

When I knocked at the office door and listened for the gruff "come in" before entering, I was surprised to find Ms Finch was talking to a gentleman; he nodded at me as I moved to pass him and I gave him a cursory glance and bobbed my head in response.

"What can I do for you, Lottie?" she asked in a voice I'd never heard her use before, it was kind of friendly, so not what we at the orphanage were accustomed to.

I glanced at the man quickly and back to Ms Finch, obviously not wanting to tell her something so personal in front of a stranger and a male at that.

She raised her eyebrows slightly, and I knew I'd have to tell her. "Ms Finch, remember when I came to you about Alice that night?" I watched her eyes widen, "Well, I've had the same thing happen to me." I told her in the most secretive way I could.

She smiled at me and then at the man, "We'll have to move your stuff to the other room, Lottie, go and gather your stuff. I'll be down to settle you in shortly."

As I turned to leave, the gentleman stopped me with a hand on my arm. "Hello, Lottie," he said, "I'm Mayor Talbot, and I look forward to seeing you again soon." Pulling my arm away, I frowned at him, the way his eyes roved creeped me out a little but I gave a quick smile and scurried away.

Quickly running down the hall, I flung open the door to the 'left' room and went to Chi's cage. "Hey pretty girl," I said as I poked a finger through the cage for her to rub her head against, "We are moving out." I quickly collected my school books, Sunday smock and Chi's cage and walked excitedly from my old dormitory room, eager for the new adventures that awaited me in the room opposite.

The 'right' room was vastly different from the camping style room I'd lived in for the last two years. The room was dissected by curtained off alcoves, each of which contained a single bed and a dresser. Once Ms Finch had shown me to my cubicle, explained the new lesson time-table and slapped a list of rules on the bed and stated that no girl was to visit another's cubicle for *any* reason, she left me alone in my new space.

Chi seemed a little agitated as she paced back and forth on her wooden perch and seeing as I was alone, I decided to open the cage for a while and watched with a smile as she hopped onto my waiting digit and fluffed her growing wings, enjoying the freedom as she stretched them out wide with no bars to impede her. She flapped a few times before half falling, half fluttering on to my bed and then down to the floor and running across the hardwood floor. Before I knew it, she was under the curtain, and I almost panicked thinking I would have to break the rules and go into the next cubicle to retrieve her, but at the last moment her head appeared and as I called "Chi, come here baby," she did her funny wobbly hop - skip back to my bed. Leaning down, I held out my hand, and she climbed up and dropped an earring onto my palm. "Naughty Chi, you stole it," I chided and held her toward her cage where she jauntily climbed back onto her perch. What was I to do with the stolen bounty? I couldn't go in and replace it, and I certainly didn't want to get Chi in trouble for roaming the room. I held the earring up to the cage-bars and said: "what shall I do with it now, Chi?" And almost like she understood, she waddled to the bars and took the loot in her beak and hid it beneath the newspaper, which I used to line her tray, and was now shredded in a corner. I chuckled, that worked for me.

Chi became quite the thief over the next few days when we were left alone in the dorm room and told to study the book Ms Finch had sent in. I was happy to read why I had been bleeding and not have to discuss it with the crabby old bat. She'd told me I would be back in the classroom the following week after I'd finished bleeding, so I was surprised on Friday when she came to my cubicle.

"Come, Lottie, we have an appointment!"

I obediently followed, expecting her to turn into the classroom, but instead headed down to the infirmary at the end of the long corridor. I'd only been in the room a couple of times in the whole two years I'd been in attendance at the orphanage. Now, as I went in, the nurse who'd always been a little on the mean side gave me an encouraging smile which put me on guard, what was going to happen next?

"Lottie is just finishing her first cycle, nurse," Ms Finch said, smiling. "We're here to see about her injection to help her with that."

"I'm fine, Ms Finch. I don't need an injection. I had a little bit of a tummy ache, but that's gone now," I interjected. I didn't like needles and couldn't understand why I'd need one for having what every woman lives through each month.

"Now Lottie, I know needles are a little frightening sometimes," the nurse said as she began tearing the sealed wrapper from around a quite large looking one, "you won't even see this one because it goes just here." She pointed at her plump upper arse and then continued with what she was doing. I nervously watched as she held the little bottle up and inserted the needle through the cap and pulled back on the syringe. "Lean over the chair there, Lottie," she indicated the patient's hard-backed chair, and I did as she instructed, Ms Finch raised my smock, and the nurse lowered my panties just a little. She swabbed with a cold cotton cloth, and I jumped as she plunged the needle, and deployed the liquid into my buttock. "It's all done." She said as she pulled the needle out and quickly pressed hard on the injection site to stop it bleeding. "Good as new!" Ms Finch took me back to my room and looked over my little cubicle.

"Welcome to the senior's room, Lottie." That sounded funny in my head after two years of calling it the 'right' room compared to the 'left' which I'd recently vacated. "When our girls become women by having their first menstrual cycle, they're moved from the junior room for more privacy and other … perks. I'll send you down a couple of new dresses and boots for your first adult Church outing on Sunday." She stared at Chi in her little cage, "And be sure that bird is kept clean and, in her cage, or I'll have to take her out of here." Lose Chi, no way.

"Yes, ma'am, I'll keep her clean and locked in her cage." I smiled lovingly at my pet and turned to Ms Finch "I always do." I lied through my teeth.

Once the old battle-axe had left the room, I opened Chi's cage. "Come on, baby," I murmured as she stepped onto my hand. "Let's clean some of this paper up." Removing a handful of old, shredded paper, littered with poo and food crumbs, I was surprised to discover that the amount of bootie that Chi had been stealing was growing into quite a tidy little pile. I wondered, not for the first time, how the other girls had come to have personal property, maybe they came in with it like I'd come in with my little suitcase. Did that mean I may yet be given my belongings back? I could only hope.

On Sunday morning, I awoke to Ms Finch's voice in the dorm room and staggered sleepily from my bed and drew back my privacy curtain.

"Remember girls, best behaviour at Church, big smiles and no talking."

"Yes Ma'am," they all chorused before heading down the centre of the room and out the door.

Ms Finch walked towards me.

"Good Morning, Lottie. Here, these are the clothes I spoke of." She handed over two dresses, a pair of pink underwear, white tights, a lovely woollen coat and shiny black boots. "Now, head down to the shower room and make yourself presentable and I'll be back to walk you all to Church."

"Thank you, Ma'am," I said as I hung the clothing from the curtain rail and placed the boots beneath my bed before following her out of the room. In the wash area, the other girls were busy scrubbing their bodies, washing their hair and towelling dry, so I followed suit before heading back to the dormitory cubicle, and dressing in the beautiful blue dress with a daisy pattern, tied on the shiny black boots and finger-combed my long blonde hair, before deftly French braiding it and secured it with a rubber band.

The walk to church this morning was invigorating, but I barely noticed how cold it was with my new woollen coat donned right up to my neck and my new boots keeping my feet cosy, warm and dry. Like a little lamb, I followed meekly into the church and removed my coat, folded it neatly and placed it on the seat beside me as all the other girls were doing. Then we sat, hands on knees, eyes front and waited for the service to begin.

It wasn't long before I noticed heads turned in our direction, and I quickly took a peek at the congregation. Yes, there seemed to be a few people watching us, I sat straighter, not wanting to appear to be slouching at the end of the row of my well-behaved peers.

After the last hymn, with the choir relinquished by the wave of the Vicar's hand; most of the congregation quietly stood and left through the side door of the church. I watched in surprise as several couples came forward; it was obvious from their clothing; they were all well-to-do. The men wore expensive-looking suits, collard jackets neatly buttoned over crisp white shirts and black ties, with a perfect crease pressed down their trouser leg, and the women bathed in jewels, fur wraps hiding their silky blouses, tucked into designer pants and their leather, fur-lined boots completed the ensemble. Why on earth would they be staying behind? The women stopped at the steps to the little platform leading to our pew, forming a tight little circle as they chatted with each other, keeping their eyes turned away, as their husbands ascended the steps and stopped in a line before us. I glanced sideways at the girls sitting so nicely, shoulders back, smiles painted on their faces, although the smiles didn't appear genuine, almost strained, what in hell was going on?

One by one the men of differing ages walked past our pew, back and forth, almost like they were inspecting us, then one by one they stopped and collected a piece of card I'd not previously noticed on the bible shelf in front of each girl before turning and strolling back to their wives.

I glanced at the wood which shelved my bible, I had no card, and I wondered what they were for and why I hadn't got one.

"Hello Lottie, nice to see you again," said a voice to my left, I'd not seen him walk over.

"Good Morning, M-mayor Talbot," I stammered, meeting his eyes briefly, before lowering my gaze to my white-knuckled fists resting on my knee; he still gave me the creeping feeling of spiders running over my skin as he scrutinised me. His shifty eyes took me in, head to toe, leering as they paused longer than was polite on my budding chest.

I peered up through my fringe and saw him nod to Ms Finch before turning away and joining his wife, taking her arm, his fingers digging deeply through the fur wrap making her wince as he led her towards the exit. She turned briefly, and the eyes that met mine showed a mix of sorrow and pity, and then she was out of the door, and I was left to wonder what had just happened.

The walk back to the orphanage was quiet. The girls kept their eyes downcast and not a twitter was heard amongst them. The feeling of impending doom only thickened as the day wore on and I was left alone in my cubicle with only Chi for company until a bell sounded around mid-afternoon and the senior students walked to the dining room for a late luncheon; the girls barely ate, picking at their plates, but when Ms Finch informed me there would be no evening meal, I went to scoff my food down until I caught my classmates shaking their heads, and I pushed my plate away. The silence was deafening as we returned to our dormitory to sit alone in our cubicles.

Ms Finch waltzed in at half after six and clapped her hands.

"Okay ladies, it's time. Toilet, wash up and ready yourselves for bed."

I had no idea what was going on, but I followed behind like the little sheep I'd become; no evening meal and now an early wash and into our nightgowns; were we being punished for some reason?

Chi suddenly screeched sharp and loud. What had she heard that I hadn't? And then there was a cacophony of sounds, voices, loud masculine voices and whimpers and squeals. My curtain suddenly yanked open, the metal hoops screeching, and I shrank back as Mayor Talbot appeared, pulling the curtain closed behind him.

"Good evening, Lottie." He said as he sat on the edge of my bed and patted the cover. "Come, sit, and don't be shy." I eyed the hand that indicated where I should sit, but my legs seemed frozen to the spot beside Chi's cage. "There's nothing to be nervous about; you haven't done anything wrong. I visit every new senior personally before introducing you to the rest of my board of councillors." He pats the bed again, and with my legs shaking, I jerkily walk over and sit as far from him as I can on the single bed. He grins at me and my heart pounds loudly in my chest. "Ms Finch is one of our council members, and we help each other out as much as we can. And so, every Sunday the councilmen visit the senior dormitory with little gifts for you girls and a little extra finance for Ms Finch to assist in the upkeep of the orphanage." I felt the colour drain from my face, I couldn't imagine any of the men from the church visiting out of the goodness of their hearts, and as the Mayor's fingers walked across the bedspread and up to clutch my knee, I knew exactly why the men were here.

I looked up from those roving digits, back to his face. With a smirk, he removed his hand and reached into his pocket, pulling out a little black bag which he emptied onto his palm.

"I've brought you a little gift, Lottie." He held up a tiny heart on a chain. "Turn around, and I'll fasten it." Unmoving, my breath caught in my throat from the fear that was clawing at me, his brows lowered to a frown, and he made the universal sign to turn. Slowly, I turned my back to him and felt the bed depress behind me as he moved closer. The necklace appeared in my line of vision, and I felt the moist, soft skin of his fingers, touch my neck as he fastened the clasp. I squeezed my eyes closed in disgust as his hands rested briefly on my neck before those sweaty digits danced their way over the crest of my shoulders, down, down they went, following the line of the chain to the tiny heart nestled between my pubescent breasts. They didn't linger long on the jewellery, and I was suddenly happy that there hadn't been an evening meal because I was certain I would have brought it all back, as I opened my eyes and followed his hands as they unbuttoned my nightgown and dived in, touching, pinching my tiny, naked nipples. When his arms disappeared, I pulled in a deep breath, so relieved that it was over. I was a fool; it wasn't over. I felt the mattress shift and knew he'd stood up, but I was too frightened to move, to look at what he might be doing. I heard his shoes hit the floor, one and then the other and then a loud squawk from Chi had me spinning around, to discover his pants thrown over her cage.

Taking my arms, he pushed me none to gently back down onto the bed, my nightgown gaping and my young, nude body on display for his perusal. "I love my job," he said as he climbed on the bed and pushed his knees between mine. I averted my eyes from his bobbing member and found myself looking at the corner of Chi's cage and watched as her tiny beady eyes peeked around the material thrown over her.

"No need to be shy Lottie, you can touch it if you would like, I know I'd like it if you did."

I shuddered, the thought of touching him repulsed me, and I shook my head, not taking my eyes from Chi.

The bed moved a little as he shuffled closer and raised my legs, draping them across his hairy thighs. Muscles clenched and breath held, I waited, and as he speared himself inside of me I would have bellowed a mighty scream had his hand not appeared, fingers clasped tightly across my lips, I didn't need to make a sound, Chi did it for me, her screech painful on the ears, but he didn't remove his hand or take his 'thing' out of me.

A groan sounded from above me, tearing my eyes from my friend to the monster astride me, wondering if he was hurt or better still, dying.

The look on his face was a combination of pleasure and pain, as he stilled within me and then raised his eyes from the dark curls at my invaded entrance to my face and saw my pain and confusion.

"Little Lottie," he huffed out a breath, "You are so exquisitely tight, my balls are aching from the need to release, but, not yet, not yet," he repeated and took some deep breaths as I watched his face relax slightly and then he began to move, pulling back and thrusting viciously inside of me and I once again turned my face to Chi and attempted to disengage my mind from what this animal was doing to my body.

Chi was cheerfully picking at some cotton on the pants thrown across her cage, and I watched her carefully as her beak dipped into a pocket and came out with some paper, she fluttered to the bottom of her cage and hid the stolen note within the shredded nest and then back up to the cotton and I watched as it began to unravel. I had a sudden image of Talbot walking away with a hole in the arse of his designer pants, and I smiled.

"Yes, Lottie," he whispered from above me, "I knew you'd love it, oh yes." He let out a groan and his body shuddered, and just like that, he finished, slipped out of me and walked toward the cage to retrieve his pants. Pulling them on, he plunged his hand into his pocket and pulled out some notes. "This one's for you, Lottie. I'll see you in Church," he said as he handed me a £20 note and left me alone in my cubicle.

Chapter three

Learning first-hand of the corruption that revolved around the orphanage and the immoral deeds the councilmen partook, I paid more attention to everything that was going on around me. How had I never noticed such goings-on before? The tell-tale signs on the other girl's faces, the way they shuffled their feet as they walked after 'Sunday School' as I discovered they called their intrusion, bruises which appeared showed some of the council liked to play a little rough. But it wasn't just the girls I became super aware of; it was the wives. I studied them each Sunday as I sat glowering towards the Councils pew, and I counted the bruises and the overdone eye make-up which covered a black eye, a bandage or a splintered finger, and I knew these women were no better off than us. They too, were being abused.

That first night, after Talbot had exited the cubicle, I covered my shivering nakedness with the warm nightgown and pulled the blanket from the bed to wrap around my shoulders. I wouldn't think about what I'd just endured; I couldn't. If I did, there would be nothing left of me. I wouldn't cry or scream. One day, maybe I would, but not now, not today. The banknote lay forgotten on the floor as I paced to Chi's cage and let her climb up my arm and nuzzle her face to my neck, before reaching higher and darting her spoon-shaped tongue into my ear, tickling, making me smile. What would I ever do without my friend? My fingers gently rubbed the top of her head, and she ducked from side to side, being sure to get the full head massage. My other hand snaked into the tiny opening of her cage, and as I moved some of her nestings, I discovered what she'd stolen, a 50-pound note. "You little thief," I softly murmured as I bent to retrieve my own fallen bill and added it to hers before hiding it beneath the bars at the bottom of her cage where she couldn't reach it.

An idea was born, inspired by Chi's terrible case of kleptomania. This plan helped get me through the torrid hours of abuse I suffered each week. As the councilmen shot their essence inside of me at '*Sunday school'* my hand would stray to their discarded pile of clothing, digits searching pockets for paper notes, any denomination accepted. Some days I came away empty-handed, and I discovered, as disgusting as it seems, that when being fucked from behind it proved to be more lucrative as it was much easier to search the clothing on the floor while in a downward-dog pose. It was better for another reason too; I couldn't see the sweaty piece of crap that was banging away at me. I wasn't greedy, and I never took enough to be noticed, but as the weeks went on, the little nest egg within Chi's cage grew and grew.

Chi continued to entertain, as the men came, huffing and puffing above me, my eyes never left my winged friend and her strutting antics going on behind the bouncing arses.

Sunday school in session, I watched Chi as she fanned out her dusty green feathers, and I suddenly realised how much they had grown. I could no longer see the cut marks where the scissors snipped, her feathers whole, strong. She flapped frantically within the confined area of her cage, so close to being airborne and I watched her with such deep concentration, silently willing her to take flight, that I totally forgot the old, balding fat man between my thighs. She lifted from her perch, flapping hard, and hovered for a long moment and then settled again. She'd done it!

So exhilarated in her achievement, I forgot myself for a moment and moved my hips, the old man groaned "yes, oh yes-s-s." As he came, his body seized, and he slumped, slamming his full weight onto me as he collapsed. He lay so still; the only movement was his spent erection slipping from my body. I lay motionless, waiting, watching for signs of him breathing; there was nothing. He was so heavy, a dead weight, I could scarcely breath myself and the arm which dangled off the bed searching his pockets began to tingle and then my fingers found something hard, shiny and rectangular, without a conscious thought I gripped the mobile phone and pressed it between the sheet and my mattress and then screamed as I attempted to push the dead body aside.

The curtain to my cubicle ripped from its rings as semi-naked men pushed their way inside to investigate the commotion. No-one made a move to assist me, they just stood, staring at their dead associate and waited until Talbot arrived, parting like the red sea for Moses as he strode forward. Talbot stood above me, his face twisted in distaste as he took in the flabby, white skin blanketing me.

"Seems like you were too much for Conrad, eh Little Lottie," he smirked, motioning his colleagues to step forward; they pushed the dead body over the side of the bed where he landed with a loud slap on the wooden floor.

"Get him dressed and out to the car," he ordered, and Councillor Conrad Reid was dragged away by two others, his clothing collected, and the curtains closed behind them.

Chapter four

I was left alone through much of the week following the death of the councillor. Released from lessons, I used the time alone in the dormitory to play with Chi, trying hard to forget the feel of the deadweight of the man pressing down on my body and my mind. Chi loved every second, as I unlocked her cage door and helped her hop to the curtain rail, giving her the extra height, she required to get her airborne. Her wings frantically flapping as she took flight and flew from railing to railing and then back to my outstretched arm.

Removing the cellular phone from its hiding place, I snapped photos of Chi in flight, so beautiful, so free. The photos captured her essence, her joy; the underside of her wings a vibrant yellow and green, spread like a fan as she flew above me. The pictures immortalised my best friend and another idea formed. If I were able to sneakily photograph the debauchery which befell my peers at '*Sunday school*', maybe, just maybe this could be the way to freedom, to escape.

Sunday came, and we attended Church. I noticed there was no card placed on my bible stand, and as the sermon ended, the councillors wandered forward to choose a card from their chosen girl for their evening session. Not one of them met my eyes as they walked past me back towards their wives. I watched Councillor Reid's widow during the service, her head bowed much of the time, but as the other members made their way towards us, she looked up and met my gaze. I wasn't surprised to see a sense peace across her face, her expression, not one of sorrow but relief and when she smiled and nodded her head toward me, I couldn't help but smile and nod back, content that in a roundabout way, I'd managed to free this poor woman from the bonds that had held her.

I wasn't sorry for what had befallen the councillor, and I was relieved when I discovered I wasn't part of the night's entertainment, that I didn't have to accommodate the wandering hands and thrusting pelvises. With no-one requesting my services, it gave me the perfect opportunity to sneak around with the mobile device.

The girls dressed; ready to receive their unwanted, unwelcome visitors. The dorm room was silent as a grave, excuse the pun; the girls were wary, frightened that what had befallen me could also happen to them. Hey, nobody wants a dead body, naked or otherwise, pinning you down.

I was just as nervous, maybe more so as I hid the camera, powered down to conserve the battery, in the sleeve of my nightie. Chi screeched, and I knew the perps were on their way; tonight, would be the beginning of the end. I waited, fidgeting impatiently with the threads which Chi had bitten from my blanket, counting down the minutes till I was sure all would be busy, too busy to notice as I peeked under the nearest curtain to ascertain the sexual positions used and what my best shot would be to expose the perps face without him catching me. Perfect, he was behind her, and as I bought the camera up, he thrust forward and lifted his head, eyes closed, the ecstasy of his orgasm caught 'snap' and I quickly moved to another cubicle.

One more, just one more photo and I'll have captured them all, 'snap' I caught the Mayor as he pounded into Alice, his hold bruising the tender skin of her neck as he pressed against her throat to stop her pained screams.

I stayed hidden, one of the unused cubicles closest to the door allowed me to count feet as one by one they finished for the night and filed quietly out past the closed curtain. Talbot was last to leave, and as soon as his shoes passed, I stood, ready to make my way back to my cubicle, only to stop short as I heard voices in the hallway.

"Eleanor, I'm sorry about your brother-in-law." Wait, what, Councillor Reid was related to Ms Finch? No way was I going to miss this conversation. I pressed the record button on the cell, cringed as a tiny ding sounded, but the talking didn't cease. I listened and recorded.

"Conrad knew his heart wasn't good and that little tart is a real treat, let me tell you. The Council will look after your sister, never fear about that. Now, what do we owe you for this evening's delights?"

"The usual, £70 per girl, and don't forget, Roland had two tonight." I could hear the soft shushing of the paper notes as he counted, she continued. "As for Mary, she's well shot of the cruel bastard; he beat her something rotten."

"Maybe, but we'll have to find someone to take his place, just maybe not someone as old eh? Someone who can fuck Little Lottie without his heart giving out." He laughed loudly as their footsteps faded away.

I clutched the phone in shaking hands and turned it off.

Rage-filled tears dripped down my cheeks as I tip-toed down the centre of the dorm, careful that the girls behind their curtains wouldn't see my feet and finally entered my sanctuary where Chi squawked out and greeted me, 'ello',

Little Lottie; Memories of my parents were all I had left, and now the Mayor had ruined the nickname, only my Dad had ever called me. *It had started one day when I'd been late coming home from school and Dad had panicked a little bit, he'd called in his good friend and detective to search for me. I'd been watching a netball game after school, not thinking about the time and was heading home when the police cruiser had pulled up beside me and Dads voice, 'Oi, Little Lottie, where've ya been, sweetie? The nickname stuck.* And now, I couldn't bear to hear it, the beautiful memory of my dad hanging from that cruiser window would forever be overshadowed with the Mayor's face as he pushed his way inside of me. The hatred I felt was overwhelming, and I longed for the day when I could bring him down.

With the mobile phone carefully wrapped and placed alongside the banknotes in the bottom of Chi's cage, I went to bed and tried not to hear the sobs from the girls down the row. The following morning, I headed back to the classroom to continue with my lessons, my week to get over the shock I'd endured was over, and now I had work to catch up on. Ms Finch's voice droned on about civil rights, the irony lost on her, but her speech didn't have the power to hold me captive, and my thoughts drifted to the phone I'd hidden, containing all the proof I needed to end this hell. The next step was to plan my escape from the orphanage, get the evidence to someone trustworthy, but who? I knew that so many people in this town were corrupt, so who could I turn to, who could bring these bastards to their knees?

Stupid, stupid, stupid, I chastised myself. All I had to do was somehow get back to my old hometown and contact Damon, Dads detective friend; he'll know what to do. But Chi, what could I do with Chi? I couldn't abandon her; leave her locked forever in that tiny cage. No, I had to set her free and pray she would be able to survive on the outside, just like me.

Sunday's were the only day the gates were unlocked. Ironic, the Church which had damned me would now become my salvation.

Sunday couldn't come fast enough.

For the remainder of the week, I secreted bits of fruit, greens and sugar cubes in my smock pockets; I had to give Chi the very best of chances if she were to survive in the outside world. The thought of saying goodbye broke my heart. She was my friend and had inspired me for so long to be brave and grow strong, so one day like her, I too could spread my wings and fly.

Sunday arrived bright and sunny, a good omen. Racing through breakfast, I hit the showers ahead of the other girls and began to dress for church. Taking the wad of money and flattening it inside of my shoe and secreting the cell phone beneath the elastic of my panties before pulling the dress over my head. Sneaking Chi from her cage was a risky business, if she was to get excited and fly, would I be able to call her back in time before anyone saw? Holding one of the sugar cubes in my hand, I enticed her out and then hurried down the dorm to the door, checking quickly and running toward the toilets. Chi licked happily at the sweet cube without once lifting her wings. Closing the door to the toilet stall, I climbed and balanced on the seat, reaching for the tiny rectangular window and pulling the lever to open the louvre. I carefully placed all the stolen food along the sill. Bringing Chi up close to my face, I puckered my lips, making a quiet kissing sound. Beady little eyes met mine, and she cocked her head sideways as she brought her beak to my lips and copied the sound. "Goodbye my friend, be safe," I whispered as I held her close to the open window and watched as she stepped onto the sill, her beak immediately searching through the goodies for her favourite fruits. I closed the window before I could change my mind and climbed down from the seat and flushed the toilet. Leaving the stall, I quickly washed the stickiness from my hands and checked my reflection carefully; nothing seemed out of place, the phone well hidden. The only thing giving away my nervousness was the paleness of my skin and my overly bright eyes.

It was time! As we marched from the orphanage toward the church, my eyes lingered for a long moment on the bus stop. Of course, I wouldn't be catching a bus from here, far too close to stand and await the next bus, but there was a timetable attached to the post, this I could use. I entered the church and sat, hands tightly clasped as they rested on my lap, eyes down as instructed. The sermon began, and I raised my eyes to find Ms Finch, my movement had her turning and glaring at me. I mimed that my stomach was upset and held my fingers across my mouth; she frowned and tilted her head towards the back of the church where the congregation's children played, and beyond them was the door to the toilet. I swiftly made my way past the littlies and entered the restroom. I took no time at all in opening the window and squeezing myself through the tiny space, taking a deep breath as I let go of the sill and dropped to the ground below. Almost doubled over, my legs moving as fast as was possible, I wound my way past towering headstones and out of the churchyard before straightening up, and then I was off, running at break-neck speed down the road to the bus stop. A nervous glance at the timetable showed the next stop was three streets over and then I was on the move again, running hard out, past the orphanage and rounding the corner. My breath came in ragged gasps, but I couldn't stop, sure that by now Ms Finch would have checked and found me absent. The stop came into view, and I perused the timetable, the bus wasn't due for another eight minutes, that was far too long, I couldn't stop this close, I set off again, feet pounding the pavement, pushing myself on even as I thought I would pass out from oxygen deprivation. I rounded the next corner and could have cried when I caught sight of the bus pulling into the stop ahead of me. I waved my arms frantically and ran harder than ever, arriving at the bus as the door was beginning to close.

"Wait!" I wheezed, body bent, hands on my knees as I fought the dizziness, gasping, filling my lungs with some much-needed air. Quickly reaching for my shoe, I slipped it off, withdrew £50 and slammed my heel back into place. The door shut and re-opened and I staggered up the steps, holding the money out to the driver.

"Does this bus go to the central station?" My voice rushed out on an outward breath.

"Sure does, love." He replied and took the note and counted the change back into my palm.

I nodded my thanks and walked to the nearest empty seat, shuffling my bottom closer to the window, hand up to hide most of my face as I scanned the streets as the driver released the brake and pulled away from the curb. Eight stops later and we arrived at the station where I thanked the driver and left the vehicle. Now I had to find the next bus home.

Keeping my head low, I studied the routes, checked the times and cost before disappearing into the restroom and once again removed my shoe and counted out the money I'd need for the journey, adding an extra £20 in case I needed a drink or something to eat; although, right at this moment, my stomach was clenching so badly from sheer nervousness that I wanted to throw up. I took the phone from its hiding place and decided to carry it as I'd noticed others doing.

The ticket lady barely raised her eyes as I requested my one-way ticket, she simply barked out the price, and I handed her the notes. I watched her through the curtain of my hair as she counted them out and then handed me a few pennies in return along with my ticket home. Now it was a waiting game, would the bus arrive before the councillors or police came looking. Watching the clock tick down the seconds had me in a quivering mess, I looked at the cell phone clasped tightly in my hand and pretended to push at the screen, copying the people surrounding me. I hadn't turned it on again since the night I took the photos; I knew I needed to conserve the battery.

Tick, tick, tick. Would the time never arrive? My eyes darted left and right, searching, praying I wouldn't be recognised, and hoping against hope the bus would pull in at any second.

And there it was, the bus took the sharp corner, almost collecting the plastic walls of the bus stand. I stood, rushed to where the queue was beginning to form, standing as close to an elderly couple as I possibly could, hoping anyone who noticed me would think I was travelling with my grandparents. Finally, the doors whooshed open, and a handful of folks jumped down. I followed the elderly couple closely, even putting a helping hand on the old lady's arm as she had trouble lifting her leg to climb the steep steps. She turned and smiled her thanks, and I quickly climbed in behind her and took the seat opposite them, head down over my phone again as I kept watch from beneath my hair.

The bus pulled away, and I breathed a sigh of relief, scooting my bum across the seat so I could sit near the window. The sight of Mayor Talbot stepping from his car had me holding my breath, would he stop the bus? Was this it? After all that I'd been through, it just seemed too cruel. But the driver changed gear and the bus continued on its way. Twisting in my seat, I watched him walk across the street and into the depot. I knew the ticket woman wouldn't ID me; she had barely looked my way and if there were cameras in the station, then good luck going through the footage, because by then I'd be at the edge of town, off this bus and on the next. I relaxed back in my seat and watched as the town flew by.

Seven hours and three buses later, I disembarked and walked stiffly into my hometown, depot. Salty tears left steaks as they dried on my cheeks, so many memories assaulted me, passing shops I'd visited with my folks, my old school; it was like a lifetime ago that I'd walked these very streets, back when I was loved, when I belonged, when I had a family.

With the phone clutched tightly in my fist, I headed for the information area and began thumbing through the phone directory. Luckily for me, there was only one *Strange* listed with the initials D and G. Taking a deep breath I hurried to the payphones against the wall and dialled the number, listened to the ring, ring and then as it was answered the operators voice requesting I insert the coins, the clang, clang as the money dropped through the slot and then a voice.

"Hello, hello, who is this?"

Tears welled at the sound of his voice, memories swamping me.

"H-hello, Damon. It's Lottie, Darren's daughter!" I choked out.

"Lottie! Oh my god, where are you? Are you okay?"

"I'm at the bus depot, can you please come get me? I need your help." I sobbed in relief.

"On my way, stay right there," he said, and the phone went dead.

I sat on the hard bench just outside the automatic doors, searching the street for the police cruiser, and as soon as I saw it turn the corner, I was on my feet and running toward it. The vehicle screeched to a stop, and the door flung open as Damon jumped from the car and ran, sweeping me up and hugging me close. I sobbed against his shoulder for a long moment before sniffing and pushing back a little, not far enough to leave the safety of his arms.

"Where have you been Lottie? We came home from our vacation only to learn there had been an accident, your folks gone, and no sign of you."

"Damon, please, I need you to take me to the station. I have to report a crime, please." I almost begged, crying again.

"Come home with me, honey. Gloria will be so happy to see you."

"Later. First, I need to tell you my story on record."

Damon did exactly as requested; helping me into the car, he drove us straight to the station and invited me to take a seat in an interview room. A can of cola and a packet of crisps miraculously appeared and a woman in uniform came and sat beside me, introducing herself as Detective Miller. Damon sat across the table, unable to take his eyes from my face, he shook his head as if bewildered and reached out and switched on the recording device, nodding at me, he waited for me to begin my tale.

His face grew pale as my story unfolded, and by the time I'd finished, his brows were contorted with anger and his cheeks and neck growing redder by the second as he attempted to control his fury.

"You have the phone with you?" he asked

He put on rubber gloves and took the mobile device I held out to him and turned it on. Quickly thumbing through the photographs I'd taken, his face paled again, looking decidedly ill as he played the recording back, he looked at me sadly, shaking his head.

"I'm so sorry this has happened to you, Lottie."

So many things happened after that. I was taken to the hospital, and although I'd not been with the councillors for almost two weeks, they still checked me over, swabbing, questioning before I was released, into Damon and Gloria's care.

Damon informed me that the pictures had been pulled from the phone and printed. A few other texts which I'd never thought to go through had proven insightful to my case. Conrad and his fellow councillors had text talked about the '*Sunday school girls.*"

The following Sunday, the police raided the orphanage, the councilmen were caught with their pants down, some in compromising positions, all quickly arrested, and the girls taken to the nearest hospital.

The senior students testified in a closed court; name suppression for all victims. The photographs and recording were damning evidence, adding more nails in the coffins, or should I say bars to the cells for the ex-councillors. Ms Finch went down with them.

The wives, now freed from their abusive husbands, banded together and decided to take over the running of the orphanage; properly, legally and with plenty of counselling for both themselves and the girls in their charge.

Epilogue

You may wonder where Chi, my inspiration, ended up! Well, the day after the arrest I revisited the orphanage in the pretence of collecting my suitcase, found in the attic amongst dozens of others. Only I knew the real reason for wanting to go back. Chi, I wanted to discover what had become of my friend. My first stop, outside the toilet block, where I'd released her. The sill was pecked clean of all the food I'd left and no sign of Chi.

I prayed she survive the big wide world. I missed her! And I don't think I'd have survived or escaped if it hadn't been for the clever antics of my beautifully bright feathered friend.

Retrieving my case, I glanced down the corridor towards the dormitory which held so many nightmares; nothing could make me step foot in that dorm again. Or so I thought, but as I made a move toward the exit, a loud squawk echoed along the corridor from the direction of the dormitory. Turning, I looked at the tiny window above the dorm door and to my utter amazement saw a flash of green. I dropped the case and ran; throwing the door wide and spinning on my heels looked above me.

"Allo, she cried excitedly 'allo, 'allo," she fluttered down to land on my shoulder. I cried so hard as she snuffled into my neck and inserted her spoon-shaped tongue in my ear, and then I was laughing, laughing so hard the sound echoed down the empty corridors. We had survived, both flown the coop and returned to find each other. I walked from the building with Chi on my shoulder and neither of us ever looked back.

I wrote 'Chi" as part of an Inspirational anthology for a book signing event, Wham Bam Author Jam, organised by a good friend, the proceeds of the book went to help fund 'mental health.'

It was in the letterbox

Plucking the delicate, black rose from the letterbox and absently stroking the silken petals as I lifted it to my face to inhale the floral aroma, I daydreamed slightly of catching Simon in the act of delivering this exquisite beauty for me to find.

Quickly my fingers fumbled a thank you with a kissy heart face text, only to stop short when the 'ping' – reply came "Not me babes, you got a secret admirer? Should I be worried?" I glanced around me suddenly feeling the hairs on the back of my neck stand to attention, seeing nothing I hurried inside. Snatching a piece of paper, I pencilled a response.

'Thank you for the rose, but I'm in a happy relationship.' Then with a quick check that I was alone, I thrust the note into the letterbox and pushed the arrow skyward, showing there was something to collect.

I watched from behind the curtains for over an hour, but the box remained untouched. Feeling a tad foolish, I left the window and continued with my day, but as I passed less than an hour later and saw the arrow pointing down, I knew someone had retrieved my note.

I scurried to the box, and sure enough, the paper was gone and in its place a small velveteen pouch; searching the street and again seeing nobody, I took the pouch inside and pulled the thread sealing it closed and shook the contents into my palm. A tiny crushed-diamante covered locket caught the late afternoon sun as the heart-shaped necklace threw prisms of colour dancing across my wall.

Sadly, I replaced the beautiful jewel-encrusted gift in the purple pouch, and as I did, my fingers brushed a piece of paper which I pulled free and opened. "I give you my heart, with Love".

I turned the paper over and penned a note back. 'My heart is held by another, please, no more gifts' and I snuck back to the letterbox and lifted the arrow. A light tap on my shoulder had me screaming as I spun, hand raised to attack when Simon took me in his arms, and shakily, I wrapped my arms around his waist as he led me back inside.

"You scared me," I told him and explained the latest developments with my stalker.

"I should go and check around for you, babe," he said and stroked my hair back from my face, "I don't like to see you upset and frightened."

"Be careful," I said as I locked the door behind him. Glancing one more time at the letterbox, I noted the arrow pointed to the dirt; my stalker had already been and collected. Drawing the bolt and turning the key I eased the door open then sprinted to the box, grabbed an envelope and sprinted back inside quickly locking myself away.

"If he holds your heart captive, I'll release you, all my love xx."

Thank-god, he was going to release me, leave me alone. Happy that the message had sunk in, I texted Simon that all would be well.

The following morning I danced around my room throwing on my dressing gown and slippers before heading to the kitchen, popped the kettle on then walked to the letterbox. Pinned to the arrow was a note, and instead of touching it, I bent slightly to read the words, "as promised, I released your heart".

Apprehensively I opened the letterbox and pulled toward me the box, removed the lid and dropped to my knees as I saw what lay inside. A glistening, blood-soaked heart and beside it lay Simons phone.

(Writers group assignment – It was in the letterbox)

I had a dream.

The world spun backwards on its axis, reversing the hands upon my clock
Faster than a dragster racer, when released from wooden chocks
The future now unheard of, just a word, it's nothing more
As the past becomes the present, and we find ourselves at war
Although the sun still rises, and the moon sits in the sky
All around are battle sounds that make me want to cry.
Cyberspace is incomprehensible, Computers, television unseen
But I vaguely recall what it was like, from whence I came in two-oh-nineteen
Unbelievably it's no different, as I take a look around
For the hatred, and the hunger, everywhere is found
The guns are somewhat larger but with a lower killing rate
And orphans, starving children huddle, in such a sorry state
Black and white are warring, the same as in my time
And religion still the focus, to which God to build a shrine?
A child dies, and a mother mourns, the father takes a bottle
Drunk with grief from life unfair, his wife he then does throttle
It seems that life's an endless coaster, which we are bound to ride
Promises, all broken, unfulfilled, for time has lied.
Hatred, war, famine, unrest, this life should seem deranged
I had a dream; Is the past today? Because honestly nothing's changed.

(Writers group assignment – I had a dream)

Beat It!

I waved my hands frantically to get her attention. Damn iPod, she was going to get herself killed I thought, the irony of it makes me want to choke. And who on earth wants to die with Michael Jackson screaming in your ears? "Jamie," I yelled at the top of my voice, arms waving like a windmill now, panic taking the place of my irritation. The train was close, too close, and I knew I was too far away.

I stood and watched; deafened by the loud rumbling of the engine tic tacking along the rails. The backwash of wind lifted her hair, and she laughed gleefully as she waved at the terrified, looking passengers staring at the stupidity of this child.

Once the train had passed, she turned to me with a huge grin that told me she'd known I was standing watching; it was a twin thing, she always knew.

"Wow, that was an adventure," she said as she drew closer to me. I found myself shaking both with fear and anger. She was barely home from the hospital. She should be resting. But no, she was out searching for adventure; why would I think she would be doing anything different?

The chemotherapy made her nauseous, her hair was so much thinner now than what it was, and we all knew the treatments weren't working. The cancer was strong, but for now, Jamie's mind, if not her body, was stronger and she resented being held back.

Jamie and I were identical in so many ways, and yet totally opposites in others. She was a daredevil, an adrenaline junky, whereas I was scared of my own shadow, but Jamie involved me in all her adventures, willing or not.

Last year it had been crazy sports things; I vividly remember how I spluttered and spat freezing water from my mouth as our much too tiny canoe was bashed around in the surging white waters of the river. No sooner had I gotten over that living nightmare that I found myself hanging from a skinny rope as I was lowered over the side of a cliff to abseil to the distant beach below.

Then there were the silly dares she made for herself but always took me along for the ride. Like the day she decided to attempt a motorway crossing; it was a freaking six-lane motorway; no pedestrians allowed. She took my hand tightly in hers, and we skipped and ran our way through the cars, trucks and motorcycles, many of which honked horns at us and had their owners cursing us through the open windows. We made it across alive only to run and tumble down the embankment on the other side and lay laughing like crazy people. Then we rose and walked back to whence we came, through the pedestrian tunnel, built specifically for getting people safely from one side of the motorway to the other without having to fend off oncoming traffic and crazed horn honkers.

Or the time she found the old swing tied to the branch of a weeping willow overhanging the river and since she couldn't reach it from the land had us both fighting our way through the heavily laden branches to reach it. Consequently, she got the swing, and I fell from the branch into the water, coming to the surface spluttering, only to find her swinging herself back and forth above me, laughing hysterically, before she jumped clear of the water, landing on the soft mud beneath the tree and offering me a hand out of the cold water. So many adventures!

We stood face to face now, once so alike we could mirror each other and believe we were indeed one person until cancer reared its ugly head! Jamie was skeletal looking now. The chemo had taken its toll, and she found it difficult to keep food down. My skin glowed pink with health, and my long hair grew nearly down to my bottom; her hair, what was left lay dulled and lank; her eyes no longer sparkled, clouded from pain as the disease continued to eat away at her.

She entwined her arm with mine pulling me in the direction of home.

"Come on," she said, "it's getting cold." The sun beat mercilessly down from high above us, and I knew the temperature must have been in the high 20's but said nothing as I walked alongside her.

"Death is a highway, Jess," she suddenly said to me. "One to walk along until you find your off-ramp." I couldn't answer her, just shook my head so she'd know I didn't want to discuss it.

We'd barely made it through the front door when Jamie collapsed. I caught her as she fell and screamed for our parents, who quickly appeared from the kitchen. Dad gently picked her up and carried her into our bedroom, laying her on the bed as Mum hurried to the phone. I could hear her, just outside the door urging the Doctor to hurry. Once she hung up the phone she came back into the room and with a fearful look at Dads face, she sat on the edge of the bed, her hand firmly gripping Jamie's as she smoothed the hair back from the face that was rigidly still.

I didn't know what to do, where should I be standing, what should I be doing?

I moved to the opposite side of the bed to where my mum sat and saw her face for the first time. The tears rolling down her cheeks, terrified me, oh my god, was this it?

Jamie opened her eyes and watched as my mother leaned to kiss her brow, her eyes finding Mums briefly before her gaze moved above mother's head to rest on Dad.

"Love you both," she breathed.

Then she turned slowly to me.

"Adventure," she all but whispered. "The highway's beckoning."

She moved her fingers, and I grasped them fiercely, I wouldn't let her leave me. Her eyes fluttered then closed. Her fingers entwined with mine as I watched her, and in my mind's eye, I saw us walking side by side down the long road; each off-ramp we passed she glanced at but continued moving forward until finally, she turned off, her fingers relaxed, and I knew she would travel the rest of the way alone. I watched her chest rise and fall, rise and fall, rise and fall. I waited for the next rise; it never came.

I lay beside her on the bed, my twin, my sister, my best friend. I took the earphone from where it lay against her chest, flicked the music on to hear her final song. 'Beat it, beat it, no-one wants to be defeated' Michael sang, but it had defeated her, and my tears overflowed and slipped silently down my cheeks.

I would miss her always; she was a part of me; all those memories we'd shared suddenly became too few. She had been all about living the life and enjoying the adventures, and I swore right there to continue her dream. I would be sure to have enough adventures for both of us.

My daughter lost a very dear friend to cancer. She was young, energetic, and full of life. I attended the funeral of this young woman, driving a car filled with her mourning school friends, and football buddies.

Cancer is a cruel disease which doesn't discriminate, old, young, rich or poor.

A Bridal Shower

Through natures gown, I wend my way
Blossoms settle as I sway
Birds above begin to sing
As lily and leafy ivy cling.
Shimmering dew drops in my hair
Underneath suns dazzling glare
Glide barefoot tween tree and boulder
Snow-capped mountains at each shoulder.
Standing waiting patiently
The man I love doth wait for me
My smile enough to light the moon
I hold my hand out to my groom.

"Dearly Beloved"

A lonely Christmas

Robert yawned loudly and palmed his bleary, sleep-deprived eyes. He eyed the clock on the cabinet between the two old, cracked leather recliners, another quick nap; he could barely remember the last time he'd slept longer than a couple of hours. The recliner creaked as he stretched his aching limbs and pushed to his feet.

"Good morning, my love," he said, looking down to the photo album lying open on the coffee table. Rosa smiled back at him from the page.

He carefully manoeuvred around the table and headed out of the suffocating quiet of the living room towards the toilet, undoing the drawstring and dropping his PJ pants to pool at his ankles and sat, resting his chin in his hands and gazing through the open doorway at their bedroom door.

He'd not slept in their room since she'd gone. He couldn't handle the sight of the overly large bed smiling at him like a happy face, with its two plump pillows for eyes, the crease where the two mattress toppers were pulled together down the centre as a nose, and the comforter turned down into a long smiling mouth. The bed taunted him, promising a couple a good night's sleep, but a cold restless one with a void on one side for a single occupant, he couldn't do it.

Robert turned and uncurled four pieces of loo-roll as the colourful Christmas scene drew his eyes to the calendar on the wall; it was Christmas Day.

Washing and drying his hands, he ambled out of the bathroom. His slippers scuffed along the threadbare carpet back down the hall and into the kitchen; where he poured a mug full of water into the kettle and flicked the switch and then opening the bread bin, he selected two slices of brown bread and popped them into the four-slice toaster and settled the leaver down. He watched as the elements lit, glowing brightly as the other two compartments remained cold and grey; would everything always remind him that this home was built for two?

With his mug of tea in one hand and the plate with his marmalade covered toast in the other, Robert made his way back to his recliner and set the cup on the cabinet. He gripped the photo album and lifted it from its most recent home on the coffee table, to his knee and stared longingly at the photographs as he slowly chewed through his Christmas breakfast.

"Toast, Rosa. Who'd have thought toast would be a part of a Christmas menu? After all those years you'd cook us a full 'English'. I can still taste the bacon, the rind scrumptiously crisp and the over-easy eggs you'd fry to perfection." He found himself chattering to her pictures more and more these past three months they'd been apart, although, in all honesty, she'd been gone for much longer.

He turned back the pages to a black and white print, "I'll never forget this one, Rosa. The first prom we attended in our senior year, you wore that fabulous aqua coloured gown and all your friends were jealous because the colour was so different from the pinks and whites, they all wore. I was so proud to have you on my arm; I reckon I was lucky to get through those doors; being so puffed up with pride." Robert looped his finger through the handle of his mug and sipped at his cooling cuppa. He chuckled, "and this one," he pointed to the snapshot, " our first Christmas; I look a right dandy in the red and white suit, the beard looks as itchy as it felt," he scratched at the imaginary itch on his cheek, "but you loved it, so much so I found myself needing to recreate that moment for you over and over through the years, until ….. well, you know it wouldn't have worked last year, you wouldn't unlock the bathroom door."

He sighed, he didn't want to remember the bad times, they were painful and cut so deep sometimes he was shocked that he hadn't bled with it. He knew deep down that she didn't mean to hurt him, but even knowing it wasn't her fault, at times, he found he almost hated her for doing this to him, leaving him the way she had. Surely if she loved him as much as he loved her, then she couldn't forget him, forget them. But he did know, he'd read every book, every pamphlet and listened to every lecture the Doctors sprouted, it wasn't her fault; but sometimes, yeah, sometimes he felt the need to blame someone for his loss and his misery.

Robert flicked the pages. One after another, the memories flashed through his mind. He could recall dates, times and most of all, the love that flowed behind the scenes of every single snap. Here they stood hand in hand at the top of the church steps, eyes staring, mesmerised by one another; she'd looked stunning in the long-sleeved gown, the neckline a little daring for our time, but she'd always been a little devil deep down. Her lacy veil lay like a sprinkling of white snow over her auburn hair and her high-heeled shoes covered in lace with baby pearl drops peeking from below the hemline. It was sad really that the black and white photo couldn't capture the colour of her hair, how she contrasted so brilliantly against the white of her outfit; he smiled to himself, he could remember it perfectly.

His eyes moved to the next page, and his smile disappeared as Rosa smiled up at him, her fingers splayed across her blossoming belly; if only the pregnancy could have run its course, he might not feel so alone right now. The loss of their child had been devastating to them both, and it was one of the awful things that Rosa in the past year had blamed him for, as her broken memory became misshapen and her recall of the truth blurred. Robert hadn't even been there when the drunk driver had slammed into her; he'd come close to losing them both. A tear dropped, and he quickly wiped it away, he wouldn't cry, not again, he couldn't give in to the grief that would surely tear him apart if he allowed it.

There were to be no children for them after the accident, but Butterball appeared in the album on the next page. Butterball was a golden retriever, and she became the child that 'wasn't meant' to be. The photos came thick and fast as Butterball grew up. We'd snap away at the oddities of this young canine. The tumbling, the stealing, the hole digging, and when she would appear in their bed covered head to toe in mud, 'snap, snap, snap', they recorded it all within these pages; She was a huge part of their life for seventeen wonderful years and was sorely missed by both when she passed away.

He continued turning, page after page. Birthday after birthday. How had they eaten this much cake? Christmas after Christmas found their home decorated to within an inch of its life, a different tree each year until they'd finally relented and purchased a fake green pine which could be boxed up and hidden away in the cupboard.

Robert looked up, the dregs in his mug gone cold, long forgotten as he'd become immersed in the past; but now, back in the present, he noticed the emptiness of the room, the chill in the air as the heat pump on the wall pulsed, its vents dusty and clogged. He had barely noticed how grimy the place looked since that day when he'd regretfully signed the paperwork and drove Rosa to the home. He'd tried so hard to keep her with him. Alzheimer's is such a vicious disease; it devoured her memories, of herself, of him and their life together. The album he now held had become a permanent fixture on the table, a constant reminder for her that she belonged here with him, a stranger she no longer knew. The Alzheimer's' had taken her mind away, and as she became more alienated from him, dementia had taken over, and the violent outburst became too much for him to contend with alone.

Every day without fail, he drove to the home and watched as the activity's lady helped Rosa with her puzzles, or to join her while she coloured page upon page, bringing the solid black outlines to life. They sang songs and joked for a while until Rosa turned and sank her teeth into the poor woman's arm. The woman would withdraw, clean up her wound and return to the colouring and the singing as if nothing had happened; and Rosa would ask what she had done to herself, and the woman would smile and say, 'oh it was a cat scratch', and Rosa would be content again. Robert used to join in with the activity and Rosa would think he was just another helper; she didn't know his name, had no recollection of their years together and gradually he'd backed away, isolated himself and became just a watcher.

He'd wished the nurses and the activity's lady, a Merry Christmas along with an apology as he left the home yesterday knowing that for the first Christmas since they were teenagers, he and Rosa wouldn't be together. She'd forgotten him, and his heart, broken as it was could no longer cope.

If His Rosa could see their home and what he'd allowed it to become, she'd kick his butt. It wasn't a home without her, but it was still their house, and the fake Christmas tree deserved to be in its rightful place in the front window, lights flashing to bring joy to passers-by. For the neighbours and Rosa's love of the holidays, he could do this.

Rocking his chair forward he deposited the half-empty cup and album back to the table and stood, making his way to the hall cupboard and feeling along the top shelf till he located the long white box with the Christmas tree picture on the front. Dragging it down and into the living room, he went back to the cupboard for the large red sack which contained the lights and decorations. He worked diligently, the room silent around him as he brought the tree to life and flicked on the switch. The room flashed sparkling and bright from the multicoloured lights, cheering the shabby wallpaper and bringing a new warmth to the room. Outside the grey clouds moved and a sliver of sun broke through and shone across the tinsel strewn carpet. Okay, he'd have to get the hoover to clean this mess up; he lifted the Santa sack from the floor and realised there was still something in the bottom, weighing it down. Robert hunkered down on the floor and thrust his hand to the bottom of the sack and withdrew some folded red material bound with a black belt. He slowly undid the buckle and unfurled the red costume from around the itchy white beard, and the red felt hat and the tears he'd repressed for all these months erupted from within and ran in rivers down his cheeks, a hiccupping cough and Robert sobbed out his grief into the itchy white beard still clutched within his hand.

Finally, he sat, dried his eyes and shook his head. What on earth had he been thinking? He looked at the album, and his Rosa smiled back. "I'm so sorry my love," he whispered as he began to pull on the baggy red pants, "you didn't choose to forget me, how dare I choose to forget about you, today of all days."

Robert finished dressing and smiled as he looked in the mirror and scratched at his cheek, "bloody itchy thing," he said to his bearded reflection. Taking a deep breath he opened the bedroom door, the bed still smiled at him, but now it was more of a welcoming grin, he moved to the cupboard and began lifting down the presents he'd stashed there from the last disastrous Christmas. If Rosa didn't want them this year, well, there were plenty of other women in the dementia ward who would like a visit from Santa.

He turned the key in his old car and let the engine run, warming the interior and defrosting the windscreen before pulling onto the icy road and heading to the home. He loved his wife, his Rosa, the Rosa he'd spent his lifetime loving; she was still in there somewhere, locked away and unable to come out and play.

The dementia ward, he saw as he entered the building, was all decked out for the season, and he cried "ho, ho, ho, Merry Christmas" as he strode purposefully past the station and the cluster of nurses organising meds and other things for the patients, who all smiled and waved him on.

"Hello Santa," said one lady, she wore a party hat and had porridge dribbled down her chin. "Merry Christmas, Stella," he said and handed her a bar of chocolate from his pocket. One by one, the patients came forward to receive the soft chocolates or a little gift from his Santa sack. He smiled and wished them "Merry Christmas, ho, ho, ho," over and over as they either accepted his gift or backed away with a sudden change of mind. He just continued to smile, he'd been here often enough to know their behaviour by now, he wouldn't let it get him down.

Rosa suddenly appeared in front of him. He gulped, took a deep breath and bellowed "Ho, Ho, Ho," as he dipped into his sack for her gift, hoping, praying she wouldn't be one of those that backed away.

"Is that beard still itchy, Bobby?" she asked, his Rosa's eyes twinkled at him like they had all their lives, and she stood up on tiptoe and kissed him.

"Y-y-yeah Rosa, it is," he replied, staring in disbelief. That was the first time in almost nine months that he'd been called Bobby, only his Rosa called him that. He watched the twinkle die from her eye, and she walked away.

His eyes filled with tears again, only this time they were tears of gratitude and love, he touched his lip where she'd kissed him, "ho, ho, ho," he whispered. "Merry Christmas to me."

Alzheimer's doesn't only affect the carrier but holds those closest to them hostage too.
One of my children worked at a home for the elderly in the UK and discovered a number of the residents suffered this disease.
She would call home, tearful, broken as she came to terms with the people she cared for and their families having to live with this constant sadness.

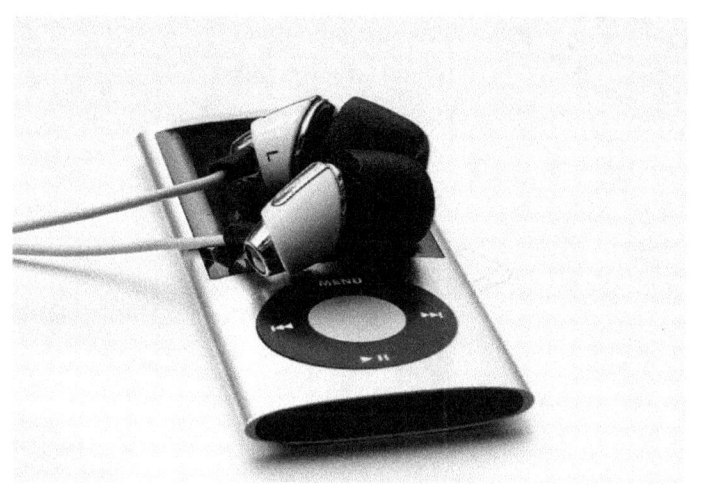

iPod

My music wasn't that loud
From the stereo in my room
But my folks kept complaining
"All we hear is boom, boom, boom."

Tomorrow, couldn't come fast enough
My birthdays on its way
Then I can turn my music up
And they wouldn't have a say.

My birthday arrived
And with it my gift
Ripped open the wrapping
Swifter than swift

There in my hand

Oh, thank you, god,
Ready for my playlists
Was my brand new, iPod.

With sounds in my ears
The volume cranked loud
I could hear my fab music
Over any big crowd.

My dad didn't like it
No, not a bit
"Turn it down!" he would yell
Like he was having a fit.

I ignored all his warnings
Leaving the volume up high.
He grounded me for a week,
No music! I cried.

He took my lifeline
My little iPod
And I hated him for it
The bossy old sod.

A week was forever
But finally, was done
And I plugged up my ears
And turned my 'sounds' ON

The music played 'quiet.'

So gave the volume a nudge
But to my disgust
The controls wouldn't budge.

The bugger had locked it
My anger was wild
My iPod's great volume
Now only played mild

… Many years passed
And iPods are no more
My grandkids have sounds
Like I'd not seen before.

I look at my school friend
Whose grown old by my side
His listening aide shows
As his hearing has died.

If his Dad only cared
As much as mine did
He would hear, without help
His laughing grandkid.

So, I'll say 'thank you', dad,
Though I thought you were cruel
Now that I'm old
I think that you rule.

This one's for Kirsten, with love xx

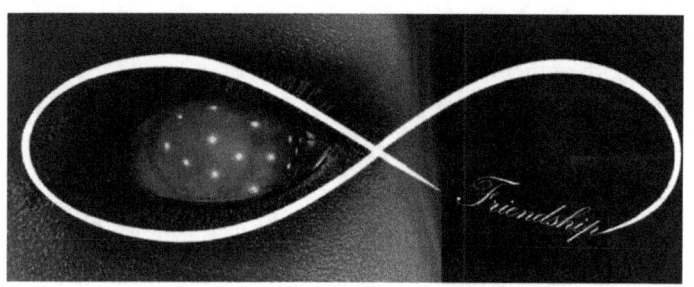

Beauty is in the eye of the beholder.

Screams alerted me to some impending disaster before I'd even hit Baker Street. Approaching the corner, I hugged the fence line, almost swallowed in the overgrown shrubbery I squinted through the leaves. A woman lay foetal style on the hard bitumen, one hand hugging her abdomen, chin tucked to her chest in an attempt to protect herself, the other hand extended grasping air, fingers reaching, searching but sadly not finding what she sought.

Three teen thugs surrounded her and as I watched one darted in and gave her a swift kick and then backed away again laughing as the woman cried out in pain and reached out in a different direction. "Bat-woman, Bat-hag," they taunted, and I didn't understand for a moment until I noticed one of the boys held a white cane in his hand. The woman was blind!

"Police are on the way," I yelled at the top of my voice and rounded the corner, snatching the cane from the surprised thug standing closest to me and moved in to help the poor young woman.

"Freak, ugly fucking freakazoid," he yelled as he came at me, fist clenched. Ducking, I swung the cane as he danced back. "Missed, bitch."

"She's called the cops, man, come on, run." Another lad yelled, and two of them turned and ran.

"Fancy a bit of blind pussy do ya, Freak?" he taunted. I spun with the cane at arm's length, making contact as it whipped his face with a satisfying thwack. Stunned silent for a second he stared at me in disbelief and then his face contorted in agony and his eyes filled with unshed tears; a long red welt appeared across his cheek as he spun to take flight, belatedly following the other two misfits. "Fuckin freak," he screamed as he vanished around the corner.

Turning my attention back to the blind woman; as she sat sobbing, a bewildered expression on her face to what had just occurred. Stepping up to her, I took her hand, and she visibly flinched until I wrapped her shaking fingers around the cane. "Are you hurt?" I asked voice soft.

"No, a few bruises, I think. Thank you for coming to my aid. I'm sorry you had to be involved." She gulped a deep breath of air and stood, cringing a little as she continued. "I'm used to the bullying, the name-calling, blind as a bat you see, Bat-woman that's what they call me. Although they've upped their vocabulary," she let out a sad laugh, "they don't normally call me a freak."

I looked at her. She was beautiful; her dark hair lay in tangled curls down to her shoulders with a fringe just shadowing her pretty, though sightless green eyes. She was the kind of person I'd once had surrounding me, pretty, sexy, but that was before.

"How far off are the police?" she asked. "We should probably inform them that the danger is past."

I snorted "I didn't call them; it was just a ruse, hoping to scare them off."

"Oh," she whispered and then in a voice a little stronger, "that was very kind of you, thanks again for your intervention. You are a beautiful soul."

Beautiful? If only.

"It wasn't you," I said suddenly.

"Sorry, what? What wasn't me?" she asked.

"Freak, ugly fucking freakazoid, they weren't talking to you, they were talking to me, I'm not beautiful at all," I whispered my voice tight with checked emotion.

Her hand reached out, fingers gently tracing along my face, showing her sightless eyes what stood before her. "What happened?" she asked.

"Car accident, fire," I said. "Kids have called me 'freak' since I finally found the nerve to step out of my front door again. I considered myself quite beautiful once, but now..." I let the sentence go.

Moving the leather strap of the cane down to her wrist, she cupped my scarred face in both hands.

"Beauty is in the eye of the beholder, and too me, your inner beauty is blinding." She smiled, sliding her fingers down my arm to find my hand and with a slight tug, we walked down the road, her cane tap, tap, tapping as we went.

(Writers group assignment -Beauty is in the eye of the beholder)

Ged

'Paradise to Rent
Home away from Home!
Pop on by and take a look
No need for you to phone.'

Ged gingerly climbed the doorstep
A huge load, upon his back
He sneaked a peek; his nose did sniff
And then he dropped his heavy pack.

His nose did twitch and whiskers quiver
At the mess, he stared with glee
For hidden under piles of shite
Was food, the price? All free!

The owner, she was sick of kids

Who'd created such a mess
She'd yelled and screamed to clean it up
She was well and truly stressed

But, for Ged, this place was paradise
In the shite that filled the room
He thought he'd died, and heaven - gone
As he fell into a swoon

Ged lived a life of luxury
In this gloomy little house
And in his room, all filled with shite
Was one happy and contented mouse.

(Writers group assignment – poem)

Christmas Sadness

Christmas lights littered the leaf bared branches in the garden. The glowing orbs which resembled little coloured eyes, blinking, waiting, watching. The colours merged and reshaped like the beads in a kaleidoscope as the cold wind snaked around the tiny garden, making the branches dance. Miniature silver bells chimed eerily above as I peered through the fake snow spray that glittered on the windowpane.

The room within was cosy. A fire roared in the log burner, creating a flickering orange glow on the deep wood panelling on the walls to give it a warm toasty feeling of comfort.

A grand, rectangular table on the far side set for five. White napkins, silver cutlery, a red Christmas candle burned in a wooden holder heavily decorated with silver-painted miniature pinecones, a fitting centrepiece for such a festive occasion.

A Christmas tree stood tall and bushy in the corner of the room, coloured baubles gleamed, and bright shining tinsel wound around and around in a falling spiral of colour, the tree was stunning to behold except for the very tip. The tip was bare, missing that something special to complete the perfection, and the lack of gifts below gave it a naked and lonely feel.

Sounds of clattering utensils and quietly spoken voices came from within the kitchen, and I watched, hunger growling in my belly as I watched the family transport the food to the table. There was no turkey for this Christmas feast, but a delicious looking crispy-skinned chicken placed on the table followed by a bowl of potatoes and a platter of mixed greens and carrots and lastly a steaming boat of gravy.

I watched as four people seated themselves, ready to eat, and I glanced to the kitchen waiting with bated breath for the fifth person to enter the room and occupy the empty chair.

From my place outside the window, I continued to spy as the man stood, and began carving the succulent bird, he served the three young women surrounding him, and they smiled their thanks, lip-service only, their smiles never quite reaching the sadness and pain in their eyes. The empty place setting drew my eye once again, and as I squinted into the candle-lit room, I realised the chair wasn't empty after all. Standing, balanced against the plush material was a golden gowned Angel; her long, dark hair streamed down her back between her sheer, sparkling wings. My gaze landed back on the bare-tipped tree; one mystery answered. The Angel was being used to fill a void, and as I watched this family pick at their food, I pondered on the tragedy which had befallen them. Would they ever smile and laugh again at Christmas?

Noticing how cold I'd become; I blew on my hands in an attempt to warm my frozen digits. The fire inside, inviting, and I reached out towards the window. Pressing my fingertips to the iced glass, hands so numb I could feel nothing as I attempted again and again to knock, to alert the family inside to the interloper in need of help, looking in at them.

I didn't understand; each night I was drawn to this house, this home, this family. What was it that brought me here? Is this where I belonged?

Night after night after night, I spied upon the sadness which consumed this family. Their sorrow never waned as they sought comfort in one another.

The seasons changed; slowly the winter relinquished its hold and spring fought her way through. The flames in the fireplace burned less and less, and the Christmas tree dismantled and packed away, yet the lights above me still twinkled, and the bells in the trees still chimed. The Angel still stood each night at the table, representing one who couldn't be there. I never stopped fighting to get inside, my hands frantically scraping at the window, my fingers still cold and numb despite the summer's heat.

I had visited them all, watched the seasons come and go. Seen the girls go about their lives yet never moving on, I couldn't understand why they continued to mourn, why they couldn't seem to let go of the past.

A year on and the room was festive once more. I stood in my normal place beside the door and watched through the window. The fire crackled, lights twinkled, the silver bells still sang above my head, the newly adorned Christmas tree took up a large space in the lounge, its silver and gold baubles glittering in the firelight and the tinsel reflected rainbow on the wall.

I was shocked to hear movement behind me. The family never entertained, never had a visitor in the whole year I'd been haunting them. A whole year! Twelve long lonely months! It was like a prison sentence watching forever the aching emptiness which had befallen this loving family.

The stranger moved passed me and knocked on the door, and as the light from the window fell on his face, I gasped as I saw the extensive scarring. Knocking gingerly and a little awkwardly, I noticed that he was carrying large bags of gaily wrapped presents.

The door opened, and I saw anger flare, though only briefly on David's face before the haunted, lonely look again slipped into place.

I moved closer, listening to the stranger as he explained to David that he'd recently been released from prison and wished to deliver his apology in person, which he repeatedly did before handing the bags filled with gifts to a silent David. Bags delivered, he backed away from the door, and head bent left the property.

Oh my god, I realised that I knew his name, I remembered him "David, David," I called to the still-open doorway. "Please, please hear me," I begged as the door slid quietly closed. I watched as he turned toward the tree, the space beneath sat empty and yet he made no move to unload the bags, to place the gifts into their rightful place.

The girls entered the room, and my heart leapt to my throat as names came to mind, Laurae, Louise and Kate, my daughters. David held the bags up. "He's out!" he growled. "twelve months and he is allowed to walk free."

Something like a flashbulb exploded in my mind, and I remembered. The visiting stranger was an unwelcome guest. It was he who'd done this to my family! It was his fault that my husband had lost his wife and my children, their mother. He was to blame for their sadness, and as I glanced toward the table, saw the beautiful doll on my seat and recalled the excitement, I'd felt when purchasing the Angel for the top of our tree. It made sense now why she had pride of place at the table.

An avalanche of memories crashed down, filling my mind. Too much, too fast. They flowed thick and fast and the pressure built in my head until finally, the memory which brought me to this place.

I had come home half an hour early from work to finish up the last of the Christmas chores, when I pulled into the driveway and startled a man in a ski mask dumping an armload of gifts that I had wrapped and put under the tree the night before, into his car. I honked my horn and pulled my cell phone from my bag to call the police.

Jumping into his car, he floored it; heading directly for me. The scream in my throat died as his wheels skidded on the ice and he barrelled into my vehicle with a resounding crunch of metal. His car ricocheted off of mine and spun, out of control into the side of the house, smashing into one of the large gas bottles attached to the wall, and in a woosh, his car exploded into a wall of flame. I remembered running from my car to haul him from his fire-engulfed vehicle, ripping the burning mask from his face before the second gas cylinder exploded, sending me flying into the front garden. I landed under the trees and watched the twinkling lights and listened to the silvery bells as I grew cold and everything went dark.

I remembered it, and now the significance of the emptiness below the tree last year made sense.

The stranger was the thief who stole Christmas from us.

I reached toward the window like on so many previous nights; my still numb fingers felt the solid pane; this was different. The feel of the cold glass shocked me for an instant as I watched David unload the bags and pile the presents beneath the tree. Then the phone rang, and I saw him pick it up, his face showing absolute disbelief, tears welled and like a mighty waterfall rushed down his cheeks. He hung up the phone and hugged our girls tightly to him as they cried and danced around the room.

And then I was crying, as he reached for the Angel and lifted her to the top of the tree. The fairy lights dimmed and went out. The fire in the log burner died, and the house disappeared.

"No, come back, please come back." I shrieked as darkness overtook me.

I awoke slowly, forcing heavy eyelids apart as the darkness lifted, and I stared above me. Blurry lights winked in time to the blip, blip from the well-lit monitor beside me, bright on my sensitive eyes. Tinkling chimes sounded from the tiny silver bells that decorated the room as someone opened a door. A white coat and a face with a wide smile peered down at me. "Welcome back, Angel," the doctor said as he shone a torch into my eyes.

It seemed my prison sentence was at an end too!

The Doctor explained how they'd had to put me in a medically induced coma to save my life and how they had been unable to bring me out of it.

Turning towards the door as shrieks came from the corridor beyond, I smiled as my husband and girls stopped briefly in the doorway and stared. Then the room filled as they rushed at me.

"Welcome back, love," David said as he gathered me into his arms and the girls clamoured around me.

Days later, I walked with the aid of two of my girls over the snow-covered path, and I pushed open the glass patio doors with a warm feeling in my fingers, the relief I felt was unparalleled.

I may never understand how I'd been able to watch over my family for the year that I slept. I'll chalk it up to the season, after all, Christmas miracles happen all the time. Right?

"Merry Christmas, Mum!" my three said in unison, and I smiled.

A very merry Christmas indeed.

I was home.

I wrote this story as a competition piece to be judged by our fellow writer's group in Methven.

Topic: Christmas

Earthquake eviction

Retired, I did at 65
And bought a widower's pad
The old folk home in Christchurch town
It was really not so bad

Just like the apartment that I rented
Back when I was in my prime
I'd saved and saved to furnish it
It'd cost me every dime.

House-proud was I with all my bits
Antiques, memorabilia and all
Now it lines my tiny pad,
Covered ceiling, floor and wall.

My memories so very vast
My life has been so blessed
Little did I know back then
That life is just a test

My chair, one day, began to rock
Not back and forth like the norm
But rather it went side-to-side
Like a boat, weathering a storm

Windows blew out, shattered glass
Bricks and dust began to rain
My sacred little pad began
To falter, frame by frame

In a panicked frenzy, I began to weave
Through masonry, all rubble
To open air, I clawed my way
Turned and found the trouble.

Never a day in ALL my days
Had I felt misplaced, alone
My keepsake memories smashed, all gone
I no longer have a home.

Many Christchurch people found themselves in this situation after the huge quakes. It is certainly a nightmare I'll never forget, feeling the lurching earth beneath us and then watching the aftermath on the television: heart-breaking.

The shadows elongated as the sun began to sink below the horizon.

Nervously Celeste looked over her shoulder; she was almost positive that there was something, someone out there watching. Not a sound, not a footstep, no rustling of the fallen autumn leaves; yet the feeling was there! The fine hair on her arms stood to attention, rubbing along the inside of her blouse. The sensitive skin beneath the tendrils of hair at the nape of her neck crawled, as though a hundred spiders had run across her back and shoulders. She shivered and ran a hand through her hair and across her neck, finding a slight sheen of sweat dampening her hand.

Her fear won, and she began to run.

Douglas watched her. Why this woman held such appeal to him, he didn't know. And yet for so many nights he had watched, waited for her to finish work in the huge office complex and appear like a shining angel to stand within the well-lit doorway, the light behind her creating a halo which surrounded her entire body, while she surveyed the darkened street, before taking the plunge and moving to join the shadows along the path.

He followed her, his footfalls silent as he easily kept her in sight; he was invisible, like a shadow person melding into the darkness.

She stopped, and Douglas sensed her unease as she began to scan the darkness surrounding her. He inhaled deeply; he was so close that the scent of her perfume invaded his nostrils, the soft floral flavour sat on his tongue, but beneath that, he could taste her fear, and his imagination went into overdrive as his senses conjured up how her skin would taste as he licked along her perspiring skin, his gut and his loins tightened.

Her fear enhanced her scent. Oh, she was so frightened! Douglas found his mouth watering as he ran his tongue around his lips and over his teeth. He watched as she wiped at her neck and he almost hissed with longing; wanting his lips on that sensuous skin. Like a snake, he tasted the air. She was about to run; this was his favourite part. He fed on her fear; it satisfied him more than a three-course meal ever could; he had to have her, have her for all eternity. Soon, he would make her his.

She ran, and Douglas ravenously gobbled down her fear, the taste sweet nectar to his senses as his fingers opened his fly and his flesh spilt into his hand. He was so close, look what the woman could do without even touching him. Closing his eyes, he imagined his lips sucking at her neck, and with a couple of swift movements of his wrist, he spilt his seed upon the footpath.

Celeste raced down the familiar street, darting a fear-filled glance behind her as she bolted into her driveway. With shaking hands, she dipped into her handbag to retrieve her housekeys, frantic, waiting for that unseen hand to grab at her. Finally locating them, they rattled as she desperately hurried to unlock her front door. The lock clicked open, and she rushed inside, slamming the door behind her and turned to flick the switch back into place. Safe. She leaned her back against the secure wooden panels and attempted to catch her breath.

Paranoia! That's what she would have diagnosed for any patients on her green leather couch had they described the symptoms she had just experienced.

Chiding herself for such stupidity, Celeste put together a pot of tea and a couple of buttered date scones on a tray and settled herself on her own personal, material covered couch; no leather in her home, it would remind her too much of her office and her psychotic patients.

She opened her briefcase and extracted four red cardboard files. These belonged to her patients she had seen today who would phone or turn up again tomorrow. Their paranoia not allowing them to leave well alone until their next arranged appointment.

Sipping her tea, she read over her notes on poor Esther. She was having some in-depth conversations with her long-dead husband, who was accusing her of poisoning him, and who was going to come back to seek his revenge. Esther hadn't slept more than a few minutes at a time in months, so scared that her husband would attempt to murder her while she slept.

The second file belonged to Joseph, with his gloved hands; thinking his skin would disintegrate if he touched another human, what a sad existence that would be. Imagine, never touching, to feel the warmth of another person.

Her third file and thickest yet was Doug's, diagnoses, schizophrenia; two personalities trapped together in just one body. Celeste had only met one of them, but Doug was traumatised by the dead zones in his life what he does when he isn't himself. He struggled when he awoke in places where he hadn't gone to sleep.

And lastly Jackie, maybe the saddest of all her patients. At only four years of age, she had been taken to live with an aunt after her mother died, brutally murdered, suspects galore but never a conviction. The aunt had been unable to cope with the death of her sister and had woven stories of alien abduction to justify why her sister couldn't come back. Jackie lived for years hearing these terrifying stories of aliens snatching her mother away and now was unable to establish what was real and what wasn't.

Packing away both Joseph and Doug's files back into her briefcase, she began to fill in new information gleaned from her other two patients, adding excerpts in the margins with ideas on how to assist them with their conditions. She worked diligently for an hour before pulling the rug around her shoulders and flicking on the telly for company. Within minutes she was sleeping.

Doug awoke in a compromising position. Embarrassment flared, and he quickly scanned his surroundings to be sure he was alone and that nobody had witnessed what he appeared to be doing. His flaccid cock lay in his hand, and he quickly pushed his flesh back into his trousers and did the zipper up. Bending down, he looked to the ground for clues, was his alter-ego taking a piss or something more enjoyable? Oh, something more enjoyable he noted from the whitish globs on the pavement. What kind of person was this man, to pleasure himself in a public place? And, where the hell was he?

The street didn't seem familiar at all, and the streetlamps appeared sparse. Glancing skyward Doug noted the orange glow and headed in that direction, for an orange glow in a dark sky normally meant a town or city centre. He wasn't wrong, in a shorter distance than he could have imagined, he found himself in a built-up neighbourhood. And even more surprising, he realised he knew the area. His doctor had a complex near here. With the location now known, he headed in the direction of home.

Dr Celeste Ludlow had made a huge difference in his life; since his first session with her three years ago, she'd given him hope, brought meaning back to his lonely existence. For so many years he'd thought he was crazy, mental, in need of a placement in an asylum. Dr Ludlow had given his condition a name, schizophrenia! Two separate persons were living in one body. It explained so much. How he would awaken in places he didn't know or how he'd gotten there. He constantly found his house in disarray; appliances switched on and in different locations to where he'd left them. It was an enigma. He discovered that the spare room which contained no bed, constantly had the curtains drawn, and the wooden wardrobe emptied; all his belongings lying on the floor. He'd repacked the cupboard many times, only to wake up and find it empty again or worse still, on occasion he would awaken within the confines of the wooden boards. It was like living with a poltergeist flatmate.

Doug would wake with his stomach churning, having to rush to the toilet or lean into the nearest bushes to vomit. Whatever his alter-ego ate or drank, obviously didn't agree with his tender stomach. Now, after tonight, Doug was positive that Walter, which is what he called his other being, (the W stood for 'weirdo' and the 'alter' was short for alter-ego) was a crazy person.

Doug had created a sizeable file on Walter. Documenting every occasion; describing the locations, he found himself, what he was holding, what lay around him. As he read through this growing file, he could see that his alter-ego didn't come across as the sanest person, and he had yet to meet anyone who had come into contact with him.

Mind you, Doug led a very lonely life. He didn't make friends easily and those he had made over the years tended to, up and disappear. Maybe those friends had seen Walter and freaked out.

Arriving home, Doug headed directly for the shower and thoroughly scrubbed himself clean. Finding himself in that position tonight, made him feel dirty, violated; was this how a rape victim felt? With tingling balls from the extra hot water and rough flannel, Doug finally fell into bed exhausted.

Celeste opened her eyes and stretched her stiff limbs, sleeping on the sofa wasn't the best for her wellbeing and was happening way too often. She flicked the television off and headed for a nice hot shower. Lathering her body and hair, she slowly began to feel human again. A quick peek in the empty fridge had her remembering she'd meant to go via the store after work yesterday, with a sigh she grabbed an apple and left the house. Celeste walked as swiftly as her heels would allow towards her office, dressed in a navy-blue suit, the white blouse peeping over the top of her buttoned jacket and showing a decent amount of cleavage. A heavy necklace hung low, dipping between her breasts. She found her fingers nervously stroking the worry stone on the end of the chain.

Daylight, even with the heavy cloud cover, made for a much more enjoyable walk and she scoffed at herself for her stupid behaviour the evening before.

Arriving at the complex, Celeste entered the elevator and punched the button for the 11th floor. The swift journey skyward ended with a gentle jolt and the mirrored doors parted. She walked along the plush green carpet, taking no notice of the expensive artwork that adorned the walls, and reached the automatic door which whooshed open, allowing her entrance to her office.

With a quick nod to her secretary, Celeste turned and smiled at her first patient for the day, pleased to see he was on time for a change.

"Doug, how are you today?" she asked as Doug followed her into the inner sanctum of her rooms. There was no need for her to gesture toward the couch, Doug knew the routine.

He sat gingerly on the very edge, unlike so many of her clients who preferred the length of the couch to relax on.

"I woke up in the park last night. I was, um, holding myself," he said without preamble.

"And how did that make you feel?" Celeste wanted to know; she was intrigued, this was new, something to add to the file.

"Violated," Doug said and then sat silent, apparently lost in his thoughts.

Celeste studied the poor man. He was so unfortunate, not only with the problem of his illness but also his entire self. He had certainly been at the end of the line when God granted looks and personality. Doug was quite remarkably ugly. Someone you couldn't help but give a second glance simply because he was so unusual. His Neanderthal type features gave him a fierce appearance, and his frame was large and stocky. His nose and ears overwhelmed his face, and when he smiled, which was rare indeed, one realised his overbite was due to his overly large canine teeth.

She thought about the file in her briefcase. She had made detailed notes of Doug's appearance after his first visit, and before diagnosis, had wondered if he may have purposely created this new alter-ego to escape the world and the cruel, teasing nature from those around him. Now she knew better.

He couldn't have created 'Walter' because he didn't know anything about him, this was her task, to discover who his alter-ego was and maybe discover how to terminate him.

Celeste suddenly realised she was staring at Doug, and he was staring right back at her. Feeling uncomfortable, she cleared her throat and wrote down 'violated' on her pad.

"Well, Doug, this is the first time you've mentioned anything sexual from Walter. I wonder if this means he's possibly reaching puberty, experimenting with himself. We've discussed the possibility of him being a child, with him removing things from cupboards and hiding inside. His way of eating foods which don't agree with you, maybe childish junk foods."

Celeste jotted this down for future thought and then watched for a reaction from Doug.

"I don't know." Doug sadly shook his head. Why was this happening to him? "I'm sorry, Dr Ludlow, I don't think I can finish our session today. I have to go," he stood and held his hand out to her. She shook his hand as she had every day since she'd known him and watched as the gentle giant of a man walked away.

She sighed as she retracted the files from her case and sat at the desk to put some serious thought into her report.

Doug left the office, his mind in turmoil. Was the Doctor, right? Was Walter a mere child? Hiding in cupboards and eating junk food certainly fit the bill. But what kind of child wandered around the streets at night? What were they missing? There had to be a clue somewhere to who his other half was.

Arriving home, Doug headed for his bedroom, flung his body down on the bed and picked up the remote. He would lose himself in someone else's fantasy for a while. Hours later his body stiff from lack of movement, he decided enough was enough. He'd spent the entire day watching someone through a camera as they acted out scene after scene from someone's imagination.

Slapping his palm to his head, he couldn't believe he'd been so stupid. Why hadn't he ever thought to set up a camera in the house and capture Walter on tape? Installing his computer in the lounge room and the webcam in the spare room, he aimed the lens directly at the newly re-filled cupboard; after checking and double-checking the camera was recording, Doug decided it was time for something to eat and headed for the kitchen.

It had been a long day for Celeste. Her other appointments that day came and went, but it was her first patient that played on her mind.

Compiling her notes on Doug had been different today due to the unexpected confession of finding himself in a compromising position. Doug had seemed different, not quite himself and she wondered if maybe, just maybe, the difference in Walter was in some way changing Doug as well.

It was dusk already when she finally snapped the locks of her briefcase and donned her coat. Damn it; she hadn't meant to stay so late. She wasn't looking forward to walking home in the dark, and she was too late to hit the grocery store, damn.

Not liking the feel of the empty offices surrounding her, Celeste silently chanted her mantra, as the lift arrived and then descended to the ground floor, 'nothing to fear, nothing to fear, nothing to fear,' it was an exercise she sometimes had her patients try. Mind over matter was supposed to work.

It seemed to be working well as she strode from her building, head held high, and her posture positively aggressive. Nobody would dare come near her when she so obviously dominated the world. She was feeling rather proud of herself for halting the paranoia caused by silly irrational fears.

As the saying goes 'pride comes before a fall', and by the time she was only halfway home, Celeste's step began to falter and her shoulders hunched forward as if trying to make herself small, unseen to anybody lurking.

That feeling was there again. Someone was watching, silently lurking. The hair on her neck rose and tickled, and droplets of sweat clung to her skin.

"Who's there?" she called voice high and slightly shaky but otherwise loud and clear.

A shadow erupted onto the pavement directly in front of her, so close she stepped back. Even with the lack of street lighting, she could make out the dark shadowy face of the man who'd frightened her.

"Doug," she said, relief evident in her voice.

"I love how my name rolls from your tongue. So intimate, how you shorten my title. Only a life-mate would utter it so. I've searched for so long." Douglas declared as he placed a gentle kiss on her fingers.

When had he taken her hand in his? Celeste couldn't be sure. She only knew that this was not Doug, the man before her was Walter. She was very excited, all fear evaporated. He appeared charming, and his way of speech was old and respectful. He was so 'not' the child that she had suggested to Doug.

"My office is just minutes away, Wa-Doug," Celeste said almost calling him Walter, as she looked down at her briefcase, her mind on the file within. "If you would care to share…"

"I do not share!" Douglas exclaimed as his eyes flashed red. The anger in his words bought her head up quickly, but not quickly enough as the hand not holding hers struck her once to the side of her head and darkness enveloped her.

Douglas caught her downward fall and throwing her limp body over his shoulder, headed for home.

Celeste groaned as she awoke. Where was she? What happened? Her eyelids flickered as she attempted to force them open, causing a strobe lighting effect. She threw her arm across her face and opened her eyes behind it, peering left and right without moving her head. She was in a room she didn't recognise, and from the height of the ceiling, she guessed she was on the floor. She strained to detect any sound to suggest she may not be alone, but there was nothing, so she slowly lowered her arm from her eyes. She screamed.

Doug was leaning over her.

"I do not share," he continued their previous conversation as if he hadn't knocked her unconscious and abducted her. Lifting her hand, he placed a gentle kiss on her wrist as his eyes stared accusingly at her. "A masculine scent clings to the skin upon your hand. You have been touched recently by another," he said.

"I sh-shake hands with my clients, that's all," Celeste stuttered.

"I believe you! I detect no other on the rest of your body," he responded.

Celeste listened to his soft, hypnotic voice and shook her head to clear her thoughts. Almost too scared to look, she took a deep breath and lifted her head, knowing what she'd see but still hoping she was wrong. She wasn't! Her clothing was gone and the florescent strip fixed to the ceiling highlighted her naked, alabaster skin.

"Why am I naked? What have you done to me? Doug, where are my clothes?" she demanded.

"Done? I have done nothing but admire your beauty. I have waited so long my love, and I wish to observe your change as I take you as my mate, unheeded by clothing." his voice was almost breathless, his anticipation so great.

"Take me? Mate me? Not going to happen, Doug." Celeste said as her hands covered her most intimate parts. "And what do you mean by change?"

"We shall be eternal, together forever, my sweet one. You will become as I, vampire!" he stated.

Celeste stared in disbelief. Was he joking with her? He didn't appear to be the funny type, but then who knows what a psychotic individual might find comical.

"Vampires are not real, Doug. They are fictional characters born from someone's imagination," she said. She used her best office voice, the voice in which to make a point to a child or a mentally disorientated person. It commanded attention and brooked no argument.

Watching Doug's face, she wondered if he was even listening as he seemed to ignore her words. Maybe it had something to do with the fact that she was lying on the floor, stark naked, while his eyes devoured her.

"Enough already!" she said and sat up, feeling a little less exposed by this one movement.

"I am a vampire!" Douglas insisted. "For hundreds of years. And through all that time I have searched for my mate. You are my chosen one and shall rise tomorrow as my eternal partner."

Celeste decided the best way to deal with the situation was to keep him talking. Was 'Walter' crazy enough to try and suck her blood like some awful 'B' movie? She wondered. Talk, she had to keep talking. Surely, her Doug, the sweet, gentle giant would wake soon and put an end to this nightmare for her.

"Doug, I'm a Doctor. Did you know I have a patient who shares your name? He is a lovely, gentle person, but he has a serious problem," Celeste didn't think she could lose her license by discussing Doug with himself. She continued, "This man suffers from a disease called schizophrenia, two personas in one body. My patient created an alter-ego to help himself hide from the world. He uses Walter, his alter-ego to walk freely, living his imaginary life without having to face the consequences of his actions."

Telling Walter all of this felt wrong on so many levels, but she had to try and bring Doug back. Celeste silently prayed that she could one day look back on this episode and find some humour in it. She mentally flicked through her colleagues' names, wondering whose couch she was going to end up lying on.

Douglas watched her; noting how her breasts rose and fell faster and faster as her breathing quickened, belying the calm her voice portrayed. She was frightened, and her scent was exquisite. How much longer could he contain himself? Why should he wait?

Douglas leant forward, taking her arms in his large hands he dragged her to him, cradling her in his embrace.

"Your patient didn't create an alter-ego, Doctor. I created your patient to escape the monotony of eternity without you," he whispered, his mouth close to her ear. His tongue lightly brushed her neck.

Celeste felt the full force of her panic wash over her. She must be dreaming, none of this was real. Vampires do not exist, no matter how much 'Walter-Doug' may believe. He was going to bite her, drink from her, and she would die. She realised just how much she had been relying on Doug to push away his crazed alter-ego, to be her saviour. But now, if what he had just said was true; this was Doug's chief character, and her patient was the fantasy created by the lunatic that now held her captive.

"No," she cried. "You're wrong. Doug is stronger. You may have created him, but you've let him take control, he is a person in his own right, a gentle, caring person. You won't be able to contain him; he will save me." She tried in vain to bluff her way out, whether it was true or not, she knew deep down that it would be too late for her.

Doug wasn't coming! He couldn't save her. She began to kick and struggle, feeling the carpet burn the tender skin on her buttocks as she writhed and wriggled to escape. He was so strong, his arms like steel bands around her. Unable to free her arms, she screamed, long, loud and piercing. Maybe someone outside, a neighbour or a passer-by would hear.

"Do not struggle, my beloved," Douglas said, his lips caressing her ear. "I can't promise that it will not hurt, but it is but one blood kiss, and then we have forever. You shall not awaken alone as I did, hungry, unloved and scared; I'll be by your side to teach you the joys of being immortal. You and I, together."

Douglas reared back, and Celeste caught sight of his canine overbite as they enlarged even further, needle-sharp as he struck, piercing the sensitive skin below her ear. Celeste shrieked in pain; voice high pitched as she felt him sucking at her neck. There was no romance in this gesture. He was truly drinking her blood. Celeste's mind flew back to Doug's comments about vomiting red after he awoke and knew this psycho had done this before. Had he killed his victims, or tried to change them as he was her, his chosen one? He withdrew his fangs and lifted his head.

She knew she was dying. Her heartbeat that only moments earlier hammered her chest from within, now slowed, as if slowly being frozen.

So, this was how death felt! There was no pain as she drifted in and out of consciousness. Her last vision was Doug's face close to hers as she was lifted and then nothing as a wooden door shut out the light. Darkness engulfed her, and she finally let go.

Douglas drank the potent elixir from his chosen vessel. His body suffused with the heat of her blood, intoxicated by her sweet scent, his loins were hard and lust-filled. Soon he could bury himself inside his beloved, his dreams finally coming to fruition. Soon, so soon, and he would no longer be alone.

Douglas well remembered his change; viciously attacked and abandoned. It had taken him weeks to understand what he was, how to feed himself. Hunger crazed and pain ransacking his ailing body he'd discovered blood was his only salvation, he'd slain hundreds of men, women and children before realising he could drink without killing if he so wished. Celeste wouldn't have that struggle, he would be her tutor, her confidant, and she would be his everything.

Celeste's struggles finally stopped, and she lay inert within his arms. Douglas continued to suckle at her neck, the pull and swallow as a babe suckles a breast. His arms gentled, hands caressing her body, touching, stroking her sinfully soft skin. He couldn't wait to be one with this goddess.

As he felt her heart falter, he knew the time was nigh. He withdrew his fangs from the slender column of her neck and drew the sharp point across his wrist until tiny blood bubbles appeared. Cradling Celeste's head, he eased her chin down and dribbled the blood, coating her tongue and watching as it pooled momentarily at the back of her mouth before disappearing down her throat. Placing his lips on hers in a chaste kiss, he lifted her body from the floor and placed her in the wooden cupboard, one more lingering look and then he closed the door.

There would be no pushing through the soil when she awoke. The modern home came equipped with a wooden box; a coffin hidden in plain sight. Needing to clean up, Douglas headed into the bathroom and began to sponge the blood smeared on his face.

Doug woke up on his bathroom floor. His head felt fuzzy, and his gut clenched. Standing with the aid of the sink, he pushed his digits along his tongue until he vomited; red acid burned his throat as he heaved. The sink took on the look of a murder scene, splatterings of red against the stark white of the porcelain. He looked in the mirror and noticed for the first time a scratch on his arm and wondered how it got there and then he remembered the camera's he'd set up.

"Time to check you out on video, Walter," he said to his reflection and headed to the living room and his computer.

An hour later, too shocked to move; he realised why his friends never stuck around. The floor beside him was stained red where his vomit had soaked the carpet as he watched Walter, the man wearing his face, murder Doctor Ludlow. He knew he had to check on her, to be sure she was dead, yet the horror of what he knew would greet him in that room kept him glued to his seat.

'She could still be alive' he thought, 'get a grip and go check.' Taking a deep breath in an attempt to keep his panic at a manageable level, he stood with shaking legs and made his way to the spare room. His eyes took in everything, his gear strewn on the floor, to the tidy pile of clothes, blue suit and white blouse with lacy bra and panties folded on top of a chair. Dragging his feet to the cupboard, he took a deep breath and opened the door. There she was. Beautiful, naked, propped up, her head held in place by the pegs attached to the back of the cupboard, another couple under her arms. She looked like she had fallen asleep standing up except her skin was sallow looking, and her chest had no rise and fall. She was dead! He had murdered her.

Fear and panic shot shivers of ice down his spine. The police would come. They would arrest him, lock him up, possibly in an asylum if the video was proof enough that he was psychotic. He couldn't be around people, what if Walter came back, what he could do to those locked in with him. No, it wasn't a question of 'if' Walter would be back, but 'when'.

Doug finally admitted, he wasn't in control here; he was merely the puppet being dangled and played with by his diabolical alter-ego.

He wouldn't allow it. He couldn't get locked up. Doug pushed the panic away and made the only decision he could. "I have to end this," he said. Which had him wondering, if Walter was a vampire, was he killable? Doug had watched enough movies to know about staking, burning or beheading. Shit! He was contemplating suicide, killing Walter meant killing himself. The thought of being burned alive, the pain of searing flames licking the skin from his bones was too horrific. A stake to the heart was too hit and miss, imagine the pain of a wooden pole piercing your body. It had to be beheading. But how?

Unable to bear looking at the corpse, Doug closed the door on Dr Ludlow and headed outside to the garage.

Tying one end of a strong rope to the roofing beam, he attached the other to his chainsaw. He swung the saw in an arc, adjusted the position and swung it again. Time and again the saw circled until finally he had the height and weight perfectly set for his neck and started the engine. The blade whirled, and Doug gripped the handle and taped the trigger down. Giving the noisy machine a good push, Doug stepped forward as it arced toward him.

Celeste opened her eyes and blinked. The room was dark and cramped. Her tummy rumbled.

Walter-ego (Alter-ego) was one of those strange stories, which just popped into my head one day and wouldn't go away. I hope you enjoyed it!

Eggs Sunny Side Up

I remember

Picking myself, up from the floor
Hearing at a distance, the slam of the door
Dabbing the red that gushed from my lip
Wiping blood from the lino, where it did drip

I remember

The skin on my face, no longer slack
Tightens with swelling, my eyes turning black
My arm hanging limply, I move, and I cry
Not broken this time, just dislocated, I sigh.

I remember

Gingerly pressing my arm to the wall

A deep breath, a hard push, a crunch and I fall
Tears uncontrollably roll down my face
I sent up a prayer that my arms back in place

I remember

I move to the bathroom; the mirror is no friend
I cleanse my bruised face, and bloody nose I do tend
With a slam of the door, I knew he was back
My poor, poor son, his name is Jack

I remember

Deprived precious oxygen while still in my womb
The Doctors tried hard, but he still came too soon.
His father's not here; we pretend he is dead
He left, once discovering, Jack's gone in the head

I remember

I walk past the table Jack's smile makes me stop
And the pain and the misery, in an instant forgot
Back in the kitchen, I begin to dish-up
Remembering this time, eggs; sunny side up.

(writers group assignment- I remember)

Sins of the Father

"I should have killed you." Molly sobbed as he removed the gag from her aching jaws. Her son, David, had pushed the grubby rag into her mouth, over an hour ago when she had first begun to scream, and secured it behind her head with a tight knot.

Tears continued to rain down her cheeks; how they hadn't run dry after all the years she'd cried through the abuse he'd forced upon her, she couldn't fathom. The uselessness of her situation tormented her, she was weak, he was strong, and he never, ever let her forget that. Her head throbbed painfully from where the knot had been digging through her slightly greying hair and bruising the skin of her scalp. The dirty dishcloth had been wet when tied, and as it dried, grew tighter; it was a torture device all on its own.

"Kick me out, will you?" David rasped. His voice was already showing signs of his, 40 a day, cigarette addiction and God only knows what other drugs he injected, inhaled or snorted.

David was only fifteen years old! From the day he was dragged from my body, kicking and screaming, his face wearing the distorted sneer, he still wore to this day; he'd been a bad egg. As puberty set in his body became heavy set, not an ounce of fat, total muscle. His eyes a gleaming obsidian black, a clear representation of the demon he was, so like his father. It was sometimes hard to remember he was human, a purely evil human bastard.

Molly had housed him, clothed him and with God as her witness, had tried to love him. Now, she just wanted him gone. To leave and never return.

Bruises, she was used too. David had covered her body with them over the years. Every tantrum resulted in some part of her body turning rainbow colours of greens, yellows and purples.

No more! This time it was different! This time she had finally decided, enough was enough, he had to go. She wanted him out, out of her house, out of her life. And she told him so! David's rage was animalistic, his fists flailing. She ducked and weaved like a practised boxer but he caught her unaware as he grabbed her hair and with a sudden movement, slammed her head down onto the bench, with a bone-breaking crack.

Pain ransacked any rational thought, and the agonising ache was too much for her to control. The light extinguished, and her body went slack.

Consciousness was slow in returning. Molly's muscles screamed, but not from the beating she'd just encountered. No, while unconscious, David had dragged her into a kitchen chair, her arms pulled back and tied tightly behind her. The sharp edges of the chair now dug painfully into the tender skin of her forearms, and her fingers tingled with pins and needles as the flow of blood was stemmed.

"Welcome back," David sneered, as he pushed his face close to Molly's. His rancid breath was almost enough to knock her back into unconsciousness.

"Let me go, David," Molly said quietly.

"Nah, I don't think so. I let you go, and you kick my arse 'outta here'." He snarled. "That ain't 'gonna' happen. This house is my home, and I'm staying."

David leant back against the bench, one foot crossed over the other, his heavily muscled arms hanging loose at his sides, as he studied the thirty-four-year-old woman for a second. Molly sat, watching those unsettling coal-black eyes and wondered what the hell was coming next. Would he kill her so he could claim the house as his own? And if so, would he make it fast or draw out her pain and fear for his enjoyment?

He grinned at her, showing a line of crooked, nicotine-stained teeth.

Inching his way past Molly, David reached for the wooden knife block situated on the centre island, this new feature in the kitchen had been Molly's pride and joy. Grasping a large carving knife, he drew it from its slot, then turned and eyed Molly, as she sat tied to her death-chair.

The fear rolling off her made his mouth water, her eyes watching his every movement, she knew he was about to make her pay for trying to eradicate him from her life. With the blade merely inches from her face, Molly's head reared back, and at the same time her foot lashed out, hooking around David's ankle and pulling with all her might as she thrust her head forward, feeling the sharp blade slice her cheek as her head struck his chest.

David, already unstable, attempted to step away from the foot wrapped around his calf. He managed to untangle himself as he seemingly danced away from her, trying desperately to regain his balance.

Luck was on Molly's side as she watched David, the knife still gripped tightly in his fist, feet stepping like a drunken idiot, cross the room when without warning, his left leg flew from beneath him. Molly watched in disbelief as the discarded rag which he'd used to silence her, shot across the room as his foot slid on the saliva-soaked gag.

The motion slowed, like in the movies, every detail, every movement, every sound as if Molly were sitting in the front row of the local cinema. His legs buckled, his arms wind-milled and then came the resounding crack as his head struck her 'pride and joy' centre island countertop. The force jolting his head back and to the side, as he fell limply towards the floor, the knife still clutched tightly slid effortlessly into his groin. Sadly, he never felt it. The impact of his head hitting the counter and the rebounding crack of his neck would have stolen all feeling as his lifeless body hit the ground.

He lay face up. Molly edged the chair closer and stared down into the face of her son. His black piercing eyes stared through her, reminding her of that fateful day almost sixteen years ago, when his father, with those same coal-black eyes, had stared at her through the holes of a black balaclava, a knife held to her neck as he pounded himself into her body, destroying her innocence as he raped her.

Police never found David's father; he never did time for his crime. But Molly had! A fifteen-year sentence.

The choice to abort the child conceived under such a heinous crime was hers, but Molly knew, she could never blame an innocent child for the crimes of his father. Over the years, she learned to regret her choice, and now, as she looked down at her dead son, she felt nothing but relief.

"I should have killed you when I had the chance, David," Molly whispered. She threw back her head and laughed till she cried. She was free!

Where does a journey end?

Pattering drips of rain cease
A young bird lifts its head and preens
Dampened feathers
A pre-flight check.

One white feather, pretty
Detaches from its host
Free falling till its captured
By a gentle downdraft
Bobbing Spinning,
A roller coaster ride.

Over green-tipped trees
Redbrick chimney stacks
Bypassing buildings and windows
Imprisoning workers behind the glass
No flight of freedom for them.

The breeze shifts and dies
The feather falls, drifting slowly
Gently downward to be captured softly
In the cupped hands of an
Excited child.
One journey ends – another begins.

Never too old.

Jacob had slept the majority of the day. He got so tired these days. When had life past him by? One more night, that's all he wanted, one night to re-live his misspent youth.

Stiffly he stood, the bedclothes dropped away from his saggy old body. A mirror showed his form, his skin a mass of wrinkles, similar to the sheets which he'd just vacated. But overall, not too bad; no large hanging beer-gut, just a little slackness to his wasting muscles.

Dressing in his old grey pants and pulling on an outdated black cardigan, yes, it had seen better days, but then so had Jacob.

The glass of water and the little blue tablet were all the sustenance he required tonight; he was not at all tempted by the half-eaten beef dinner still sitting on the table. Placing the pill on his tongue, he swallowed and chased it down his throat with the tepid water, and he smiled. He'd been planning this night for the longest time. A quick scrub of his teeth, all his own he was happy to say, and comb tugged carefully through the thinning grey hair.

At the front door, Jacob collected his bowler hat, positioning it perfectly straight as was worn by the pompous gentlemen in his neighbourhood of old and collecting his cane from the umbrella stand he exited the flat.

With one hand on his stick, the other slipped into his pocket where he could feel the crinkled notes, surrounded by a rubber-band. A smile crept to his old lined face. Tonight was the night! Jacob's fading memory had retained the address, although he could barely remember yesterday's date, yet this, this he'd committed to memory by reading it over and over. He knew the exact location he was heading. Thank goodness it wasn't too far; as he felt his old body beginning to stiffen as he walked.

He reached the tired arched entryway, in need of repair and a new paint job, and stepped inside the tunnelled area. Tapping his cane gently on the stained-glass window in the door, he waited with growing excitement.

Angel sashayed towards him, the glass adding colour to her alabaster skin, the lit lamp behind her creating an angelic aura. Jacob's breath caught in his throat as she opened the door and reached her delicate hand out, clasped his leathery, aged digits in hers and drew him inside.

Her bra and panties were floral with just a touch of lace, he could see that now that he was on the same side of the painted glass, but her skin still wore a florescent sheen, maybe the shimmering aura was a figment of his over-stimulated mind.

Ping! The rubber band broke as he handed over the mixed denominations, he'd syphoned from his pension each week, her laughter tinkled, reminding him of tiny bells, heavenly chimes.

Angel relieved him of his black cardigan and grey pants; his bowler hat stayed firm until she gently assisted him to her bed, where it slipped sideways and fell to the floor. His body almost lost within the clouds of soft sheets adorning the biggest bed he'd ever seen; it would never have fit in his bedroom.

His cane clattered to the floorboards as the bed shook and he lost himself in the arms and womanly places of his earthly Angel.

Much, much later; the little blue tablet had worked wonders. Jacob slipped from his Angel and her bed and ever so slowly re-dressed, his eyes never leaving the exhausted beauty on the bed.

Gathering up his cane and hat, Jacob left the sleeping woman to her dreams and silently left the building. Oh, what a night!

Pausing in the archway, he placed his bowler on his head at a jaunty angle, just like in his youth; this was used as a sign to all, of a job well done. His cane clicked the paving as he slowly walked away from her apartment, a smile adorned his face. He swung his free arm, the floral bra he clasped, danced beneath his fingertips; stolen panties were so cliché.

Yes, we're all ageing and sometimes the years creep up much faster than we expect. Remember to dream still, and don't be afraid to use that little nest egg to enjoy one last hoorah.

Growing Pains

A child that's growing as you are
Often wish on nights' first star
When that wish does not come true
That's when your angels comfort you.

The times you feel you're not alone
In your room, safe in your home
Nothing nasty has come to call
Your Angel's dancing on your wall.

For every one of us, I'm sure
Has an Angel strong and pure
To push away the hurt and fear
And let you know a friend is near.

A girl I used to child-mind many years ago had trouble settling into her new home.
She felt like someone was watching her; someone that she couldn't see but could feel.

So, I wrote her this poem. She's all grown up now; I wonder if she remembers.

There's an Angel among us.

"There's an Angel among us." Shay laughed and pointed.

The group turned as one; myself included, and watched as Leigh approached the waiting crowd of teens.

Dressed entirely in white, emphasising the vibrant red curls which caressed the length of her spine. Leigh wore a cheesecloth shirt, its large billowing batwing sleeves flapping as the wind caught them; the hem cinched in tight over her hips, by a drawstring which overlapped the waistband of the long flowing skirt, painted white sneakers completed her angelic appearance.

Standing before us wearing a ghost of a smile, lip service only as her smile never made it high enough to erase the stain of sadness in her gold-flecked green eyes.

"Hey," I called.

Her eyes surveyed the people before her, searching till she found the owner of the voice and gratitude filled her face that someone in the crowd acknowledged her. The rest tittered and stared.

I watched as her head bowed and her shoulders slouched, a technique she'd perfected to conceal her face behind the fall of her hair; hiding in plain sight. She peeped through the waterfall of red and enviously eyed the scantily clad bikinis the girls wore, and behind them the lads in bathers and t-shirts of assorted colours except me! I always wore black.

Shay giggled at Leigh's obvious discomfort which caused the poor girl's pale face to suffuse with colour, becoming a beacon of embarrassed radish-red, and I knew she was mine when I caught sight of a shimmer of tears in those expressive green orbs, and her head bowed lower.

Climbing the steps of the bus, I felt my elbow grasped, and Shay's voice whispered beside my ear.

"Raze, come and sit with me!"

I gave her a lazy smile, inclined my head as thanks for the invite, but still slipped into the screamingly empty seat beside Leigh. Shay sniggered, thinking I was continuing the bullying; teasing, making Leigh self-conscious and uncomfortable. She couldn't have been more wrong!

Throughout the entire journey, Leigh never once lifted her gaze from the grimy shoe-scuffed floor between her feet, not a sound came from between her lips, she seemed oblivious to the jesting, laughing kids who surrounded her.

I joined in the frivolity, feigning interest in the crowd of bully's who went out of their way to make themselves bigger, better, by belittling the weaker and downtrodden; but my attention never wavered from the cloud of self-loathing and sadness radiating from the beautiful young woman beside me. Her hands were ever moving, with nervous agitation. My arm accidentally brushed hers as we hit the speed hump bisecting the road from the beach, and her eyes rose to mine for a mere second before returning their gaze to the grimy floor, but it was long enough for me to see that resignation had replaced the hurt and the sadness.

Once the bus pulled into the parking bay, there was a mad scramble for the door as the kids rushed toward the sandy beach and cooling spray of the crashing waves.

I emerged slowly, into the humid atmosphere, the heat taking my breath after the coolness of the air-conditioned vehicle.

Squeals of delight and feigned horror as the waves chased and caught a handful of the girls, the cold water quickly soaking their heated bodies and had their unblemished skin glistened with salty droplets of water. The boys were quick to get in there and play the hero, picking up the squealing females and depositing them back to dryland.

Glancing back, I watched Leigh climb ever so slowly down the steps of the bus, and the door shushed closed behind her.

Some may take the look of apprehension on her face for fear, but I knew that Leigh wasn't frightened of the rising tide, no, there were much bigger horrors for her to face before she even stepped into the waves.

Leigh slowly unbuttoned her skirt and let it drop to the sand. Draping her towel around herself, attempting to shield her body, she removed the cloth shirt and kicked off her sneakers, checking on the frolicking girls, watching them scream and cling to the good-looking lads. Once she was certain that nobody was watching, Leigh allowed her towel to drop.

Her one-piece suit, with the addition of a slight ruffle, completely covered her torso. The style would have been becoming on a toddler, but it was not the suit that made her wait for the group to become preoccupied, before stripping down. It was the extremely large deep-purple birthmark which swept across her shoulders, down her back and traversed her arms as far as her elbows.

"Here comes the purple people eater," screamed Shay spitefully.

Silence, as everyone stopped dead and turned to stare.

"Oh my God, and what the hell is she wearing?" Janice laughed.

I watched Leigh carefully. The apprehension vanished, the humiliating red that had painted her face drained, leaving her pale and drawn. A slight shiver ran over her skin, and even beneath the scorching sun, goose flesh covered her body. Those green eyes scanned the bully's spread before her, and a look of determination coated her face. Those nervous hands finally stilled.

Marching down the sand, she passed the ogling, taunting teenagers and strode into the water. Diving over one large wave and into the next, she swam deeper; treading water, she looked back at the distant beach. Nobody watched, nobody cared enough. She didn't fit in with the kids, and she never would.

Her legs ceased their jogging and Leigh sank. The beach quickly concealed by the cerulean blue ocean as a strong under-current caught her body and dragged her deep, deeper. I watched her closely as she offered no resistance, her face peaceful in her decision.

Leigh opened her eyes to the murky water as I took her hand in mine and held it tightly. My shirt vanished, and I unravelled my black-veiled wings, understanding flared instantly in her eyes, gratitude and relief transformed her normally sad smile when she realised, she wouldn't die alone.

"There's an Angel among us." Shay had said. And she'd been right!

My name is Raze, short for Azrael.

And I always wear black.

B-b-bullied

I'm s-s-sorry that I st-st-stutter
I know it's r-really bad
The kids at s-school all t-tease me
It r-really makes me s-sad

I t-try so hard t-to act all c-cool
When the p-popular k-kids come by
They never g-grow tired of m-mimicking me
It m-makes me want to c-cry

Why do b-bullies have to b-be so cruel?
I never d-did them harm
With smokes piled high upon the seat
I drove out to the farm

Climbed up on the tractor seat
I lit every single smoke
My head begins to spin, such speed
And without a stammer, I spoke

"Goodbye cruel world, see you in hell
For me, both are the same"
Petrol tank plus tiny flame
"I hope you bullies burn with shame!"

I despise bullies.
Cowardly, chicken-shit people who get off on humiliating and
hurting others.

I hope every one of them burns with shame for what they've put their victims through.

Tobias

Dragging one leg; muscles rendered worthless from a long past accident, made the short journey painfully slow. Tobias found his crutches sinking deep into the loosely shifting stone on the old rail yard.

His cap pulled tightly down over his head, helped shield his heavily lidded eyes from the dying rays. An old brown cardigan hung from his wasted body. Eighty-three years old; where had those years gone? How long had the man in the mirror reflected the angry, abused and broken man he'd become?

The railway tracks, old, red-rusted lay before him. The heavy wooden sleepers cracked and splintered from years of snoozing beneath the scorching sun.

Many years had passed since the last train had travelled, clickety-clack, clickety-clack along these old iron grids.

His spine almost creaked as he slowly bent forward and placed his crutches upon the weather-worn stones and then eased his tired, old body down until he was seated upon the sun-warmed girder.

His gaze travelled to the far distance where the two lines, like a pair of legs, seemed to meet, becoming one body. The trees had grown around them, making them almost impossible to see in some areas. Only the setting sun, in shades of hazy pinks, orange and reds caused the iron to glint, proving they were still there, still intact. After all these long, long years; yes, they were still intact.

Tobias sat for a long time, staring. His back ached, and his useless emaciated limb lay uncomfortable against the unforgiving ground. Yet he refused to stand to relieve his discomfort, refused to leave until he was ready. He sat in this exact location, his shoulders tense and expectant. The aroma of Eucalyptus leaves overpowered the oily tar smell of the railway sleepers, and Tobias breathed deep, slowly letting the tension die away as he allowed himself to enjoy the relaxing scent. The quiet enveloped him with only minute sounds of tiny animals scurrying, finding food before the darkness would send them scuttling back to their little holes in the earth.

Closing his eyes, he let himself go, back, back into the past forever engraved in his mind; it came to life like a movie playing on the insides of his eyelids.

The vision, so real that Tobias could feel the sun scorching the dark bare skin on his back could almost feel again the sweat that glistened on his shoulders and trickled down his sleek muscular frame to drench the overalls tied at his waist. The legs of his pants torn, streaked with rusty red blood where he'd wiped work-worn hands, blistered and split, the ooze staining the rough material.

The shackle around his ankle made movement awkward, as Tobias, alongside the other inmates, carried the sleepers and rails, nailing them in place.

This had been his life if you could call this 'life'.

For the first few months, each drop of sweat that fell was guilt and grief for Jacob, his best friend.

The quarry was unsafe! Everyone knew it. He should have known better than to attempt the climb, but the saying goes, 'rules are made to be broken'. His friend, Jacob, had followed as he always did, even though Tobias has told him it was too dangerous and had urged him to stay away. Tobias conquered the treacherous shingle slide, reached the top ledge and hauled himself over the lip. He stood up and with arms spread wide, and took a sweeping bow to his imaginary audience.

Imaginary, no! There was someone watching; watching with hatred in his eyes as Tobias climbed from the pit and took his bow to the heavens. Continued to spy as his brother, Jacob followed Tobias like a little lamb. He saw Jacob's arm appear over the lip of the mound as he clawed his way to the summit, his brother leaning heavily on the shoulder of the pit as the ground gave way. He bore witness as Tobias dropped to the ground, leaning, scrabbling to grasp the outstretched hand but with only the barest touch of fingertips, Jacob disappeared with a shriek.

Within the cold brick walls of the courthouse, Tobias sat grief-stricken as his best friend's brother took the stand to testify. Face white against the dark shirt and tie but gaining a pink hue as he lied. He described in detail how he'd followed his brother, Jacob and watched as Tobias had climbed from the gaping pit and then turned and pushed his companion to his death. Judge and Jury, white men all, turned to the dark-skinned, seventeen-year-old boy and brought the gavel down.

"Guilty!" And Tobias was taken away.

Twenty-four years. Sweat dripped into the dirt; cementing his hatred for those who believed a lie; for the white people who incarcerated him in this hellhole and for the white guards who wielded batons simply because they could. How many times had his back worn purple bruising from the long wooden baton for simply daring to look up towards the freedom of the sky? With backs bent, muscles screaming, the prisoners dug trench after trench, settling the heavy sleepers before adding the shiny iron rails and the railroad spike hammered in place.

Day in, day out. Until the accident.

Tobias gripped his end of the rail-sleeper, the heavy rectangle of wood held square above the perfectly sized bed they'd cleared of stones and debris. If it wasn't lined squarely the first time a nasty blow across the shoulders was what you could expect from the guards. Three men, to lift, hold and place the solid wood into place. Joseph, the middle man of our trio, cursed as his sweaty hand slipped and the wood jerked as he fought to correct his grasp, the law of silence broken, as the white bastard standing behind him heard the curse. Tobias hadn't time to call a warning, as the baton was raised and brought down hard upon Joseph's shoulder. What happened next was a blur of action. Joseph's body lurched, and the sleeper was suddenly too heavy, it dragged skin from their hands as it twisted and began its descent. Unable to manoeuvre with ankles interlocked by the shackles, Tobias found himself dragged by the other two men. Down he went. His ankle wrenched and the chain cut bone-deep as the 200-pound wooden railway crosstie landed, crushing his leg beneath it. Tobias screamed in agony as the other dark-skinned men leapt forward to lift the sleeper from him. Blood soaked his trouser leg as his fellow prisoners dragged him away from the track and dumped him unceremoniously into the back of the old pickup truck, used each morning and night to transport the prisoners. Tobias was bumped and jostled on the old wooden planks as the driver, with no real thought to the patient in the back, drove at breakneck speed over the rocky ground.

Amputation would have been the cleanest way of fixing the leg. But no, after cutting away the tattered pants and finding jagged bone protruding from the skin, the prison Doctor grasped the leg and dragged the bone into place. Grinding the shards and catching nerves, he patched up the shattered leg and then left.

Four months later, a lifetime to Tobias who had shaken and shivered through shock, pain and infection, was released from the hospital wing, handed a pair of crutches and put to work in the kitchens where once seated on a stool, he stayed the entire day.

Once his prison sentence ended, his life sentence began. Nobody wanted to employ a black ex-con with an emaciated leg. He was living in a tiny council flat with a meagre disability allowance from the government. His burning hatred kept him imprisoned, and his hardened heart ensured he was friendless and lonely.

Not one card adorned his grubby flat; not one well-wisher came with a candle on a cake. Tobias awoke on his eighty-third birthday the same as he had awoken all the birthdays before, alone.

As he stared in the mirror, something finally snapped. It was time, time to face his past, to dispense of his ghosts. He needed to relinquish the hatred.

Dressing in his old drab brown cardigan, he jammed his cap tightly over his sparse grey hair and let himself out the door. Hobbling his way to the bus depot, he clambered with great difficulty up the steps and through the doors which swished closed behind him. He sat away from the other occupants and *stared at the passing scenery without really seeing at all. As they approached the old, unused station he stood and pulled on the 'Emergency' cord, the bus driver reluctantly stopped, opened the doors and watched with disinterest as the old man left.*

Half a mile was the equivalent to running a marathon to the disabled Tobias. But determination had pushed him to his destination.

A touch to his shoulder made him jump and brought him out of his reverie, as a young man spoke.

"Excuse me, are you injured? Sir, can you hear me?"

Tobias's old tired eyes squinted through the gloom at the two teens standing before him.

A hand settled on his shoulder, a gentle touch, not something he'd come to expect from this location.

"Sir, can we help you?"

The voice bought him back again. The lad had called him 'Sir'. He'd never been spoken to with that kind of respect in all his days.

Tears, damned for over sixty years threatened and as he stared up at the proffered hand of the smiling young man, they overflowed, streaking down his wrinkled face and falling onto the stones and dirt.

The same dirt that had been saturated with both his sweat and blood now drank the salty drops of his tears, as the bitterness and hatred of the past flowed past his heavy lids.

He dabbed his eyes with the coarse wool of his sleeve and smiled through his tears.

"That would be most kind of you, young man."

Tobias raised a shaking arm, his cardigan slipped down to his elbow, and the young lad grasped the bared, dark skin with long, strong and oh, so very white fingers.

Tobias smiled.

One person's lies can change the course of another's life. Be careful what you say.

How he must miss the good old days

It's late Christmas Eve, and the sky's filled with snow,
and Santa's packed sleigh has places to go
The grimacing fat man all bundled in red,
would rather be home, asleep in his bed

The reindeer's antlers all covered in tinsel their legs wearing
bells in a cluster
As Santa does rise, the sleigh almost sighs, its colour now faded,
lacklustre
Toward the chimney goes creaky St Nick, arthritis in fingers
and toes
Long gone are the days when he'd scuttle on down, with a
finger laid close to his nose

Too fat, too old to face the squeeze, he prays that no child is
peeping

As he clicks his fingers and teleports in, no need for quietly
sneaking
He chews crumbling cookies, all gluten-free, drinks lactose-free
milk that is sweet
He'd prefer eggnog, with plenty of rum and a pie filled with
fruity mincemeat

Tips up his sack to unload the bounty, the packages all boxed
with care
an iPod, an iPad electronics 'a' plenty, perfume and something
to wear
the gifts are so different from what he'd delivered; toys are now
part of the past
back then it was cycles, dolls houses, and balls; wooden toys
built strong that would last

Kids now, don't play, they sit on their arse, eyes blank from
staring at screens
I'd love to deliver the old type of gifts when kids played with
dolls and machines
But that time has passed, and Santa Claus sighs, his once
twinkling eyes are now dead
he looks at the window his reflection looks back, and the future
does fill him with dread.

If wishes were real, he'd turn back the clock to when children
were children once more
When he'd creep past their beds, and grin to himself when the
kids all pretended to snore
He misses those times more than anything else; time's
extinguished his magical light

Back in his sleigh, soft music does play, Merry Christmas to all, and goodnight.

(writers group assignment – Christmas poem)

Acknowledgements

To the amazing women in the Ashburton Writers Group.

To Steve for the illustrations.

Last but by no means least, a huge thank you to you, the readers.

Also by this Author

Deborah Carter was born in the UK and moved to New Zealand as a child. She is a wife, mother of 5 and grandmother to 7. Works full time and spends free time reading and writing. Favourite book genre - vampires, shifters, romance.